# ALTERNATIVI

# ALTERNATIVE MEDICINE

## LAURA SOLOMON

Published by Woven Words Publishers OPC Pvt. Ltd., 2017
Copyright© Laura Solomon, 2017

First Published by Flame Books

ISBN-13:  978-93-86897-05-3
ISBN-10:  9386897059
Price: $15

Woven Words Publishers OPC Pvt. Ltd.,
Vill: Raipur, P.O: Raipur Paschimbar, Dist: Purba Midnapore, Pin:
721401, West Bengal, India.
www.wovenwordspublishers.net

# CONTENTS

## ALTERNATIVE MEDICINE

Halfway through his second year at medical school, my brother David took a job as a dancing bear. He proudly announced his new vocation one Sunday, over one of our mother's vegan roast dinners; peppers, spuds, pumpkin, drizzled in olive oil and sprinkled with rosemary and rock salt.

"I've taken a little part-time work as a dancing bear," he said. "Just shopping malls and kid's parties. It's easy work and surprisingly well-paid. In fact, I'm kind of starting to wonder why I'm bothering with medical school at all. Maybe I could just quit and go full time as a bear. Pass me the hummus would you Mum?"

Our mother nearly choked on her slice of whole meal bread.

"A bear?" she scoffed. "I didn't shell out on those exorbitant fees so that you could go galavanting round the town dressed up as a *bear*."

David stood his ground.

"It's not *galavanting*," he smoothly replied. "It's good work. Hard graft. The kids love it. They respond instinctively to my furry paws and kindly nature. My growl is not frightening, but soft. More of a purr, really. On the bear scale, I'm closer to Teddy than Grizzly."

Dad continued to calmly eat his dinner. His wife was not quite so composed.

"Oh David," she said. "Why do you have to be a bear? Why can't you just take some casual bar work? Or apply for a larger student loan?"

"I like the job," came the glib reply. "It makes a pleasant change from aortas and tibias and fibulae."

Silence.

"Well," said Mum, eventually, pursing her lips. "It's your life dear. You do what you like with it. Larry, would you switch on the radio please?"

I did as I was told. Nothing more was said about the bear that evening.

Several weeks later, my mother found the heart in the freezer. She was feeling tired and, having come to the conclusion that this could well be due to a lack of iron, she had decided to make a spinach tortilla for her lunch. Three years previously, at her insistence, the whole family had turned pescatarian or vegaquarian; call it what you will, we ate only fish and veges. She said that fish was good for the brain; every night she gave us spoonfuls of cod liver oil. I would hold mine in my mouth, then run to the upstairs bathroom and spit it out. David always swallowed his.

At our house, we had two freezers; a small unit above the fridge, and a larger deep freeze in the garage, which is where the heart was found, underneath a bag of scallops, nestled up against a lobster that had sat there, uneaten, for the last decade. The heart was in a blue plastic bag, coated with that fine white ice you get when you haven't defrosted in a while. She didn't realise what it was at first. She thought it was a piece of old steak or liver, bought long ago, in the meat-eating days, forgotten, now rediscovered. She took it upstairs and put it in the microwave on low, stood watching the plate revolving in the glow of that dull, artificial light. When she considered it sufficiently thawed, she took it from its bag and laid it on a plate. It was then that she recognised the organ. Not the stylised Valentine's Day tomato-red ticker, with the two curves at the top, like a woman's breasts, narrowing to a single point, but a solid lump of meat, dark red, almost brown. If you looked closely enough, you could see the valves. She had no recollection of buying such a thing herself, but assumed that somebody, Dad or David, must have, years ago, purchased an ox's heart, intending to make some kind of stew perhaps, or a satay. It wasn't until that evening that she discovered that this heart was not animal, but human.

We ate together as a family every night, sitting at the dining room table. My mother thought it helped us to communicate with one another. I was envious of other families, who ate in front of the television with plates positioned on trays or, more precariously, on their laps. We didn't have a TV to watch; my father said that it rotted the brain. It was usually my mother who kicked off the conversation. This night was no exception.

"You'll never guess what I found in the freezer this afternoon," she began.

"What, the deep freeze?" asked Dad. "Surprised you can find anything in there. Needs a good clean out, that does."

"A heart," she said. "Whom does it belong to?"

"Oh yeah," said David. "I was going to tell you about that. What did you do with it?"

"It's on the kitchen bench. Is it a cow's heart?"

"No, human."

"What on *earth* did you bring it home for? Assuming, of course, that you got it from the medical school and haven't been digging up the graves of the recently deceased in order to rob them of their vital organs."

"I was intending to pickle it."

"To *pickle* it?"

"Yeah, chuck it in some formaldehyde. I thought it could serve as a kind of study aid, you know."

"Oh David. Couldn't you just have left it at the university?"

David shrugged.

"I didn't think you'd mind," he said, pushing back his chair and rising to his feet. "Anyway, I'm going out for a bit."

Our mother looked alarmed.

"Where are you going, dear? I thought we could all play a nice game of Scrabble this evening."

"Got a bear appointment," came the mumbled reply.

"At            this            time            of            night?"

"Eighteenth birthday party. In a bar downtown."

"Isn't eighteen a little too old for dancing bears?"

"They're payin', I'm playin'."

"Well, please try to be quiet when you come in."

"Will do. See you later. Put the heart back in the freezer, will you?"

He bent down and gave her a little peck on the cheek.

Three weeks later she discovered the brain in a box beneath David's bed. Unlike the heart, it was not frozen. She found it when she was vacuuming his room – she only did under the beds once a month. She knew that she should leave the box alone, yet, against her better nature, she opened it anyway. There it sat, a lump of broiled grey cauliflower, a three-pound universe. An internal map that had once reflected somebody's external world, but that now sat inert, mindless. She put the lid back on the box, put the box back under the bed.

At the dinner table that night, she said, "David, was that a brain I found under your bed today?"

"Oh," said my brother. "Thanks for reminding me. I need to get onto preserving that. I've brought all the kit home; the latex, the formalin. I just keep procrastinating."

My mother put down her knife and fork and folded her arms.

"David," she said firmly. "I know that you're a medical student, but I don't want my house filled with human organs. It's macabre."

"It's not *macabre*. It's part of life, part of death. It's the body. Everybody's got one; you've got one, I've got one."

"But what if we have visitors David? Nobody wants to walk into your room by accident and find a brain in a jar. Or a pickled heart."

"I'll keep them in the wardrobe. Jesus Mum! I know you've stumbled across these things, but it's only because you're always prodding about in various corners of the house. It's not like I leave them lying about the place. Gimme a break, would ya? Anyway."

*Scrape*. The sound of his chair legs across the floor.

"Bear gig calling. See ya tomorrow morning."

He picked up the bear suit that he kept hung on a hook by the door. A second later, we heard the engine of his car splutter into life and he roared off down the road. My mother turned to her husband.

"You know, Cliff," she said. "I really would appreciate it if you would back me up on these things, instead of just sitting there shovelling     lentil     pie     into     your     mouth."

"Don't take it out on me, love."

"But don't you think it's odd, that he brings these things home?"

"Harmless, love, harmless. Ignore it. Better that than shooting up heroin in some dark alley, right?"

He reached out and gave her hand a squeeze then retired to the living room to read his evening paper.

"It's this bloody bear thing," my mother muttered, more to herself than to me. "He never used to bring this garbage home before he had that ridiculous job." She cleared the dining room table, than began furiously cleaning the kitchen benches, as if all her worries could be scrubbed away with a bit of Crème Cleanser and a scouring cloth.

There was a femur in the medicine cabinet; it was small, a child's. It was me that found it. I had been helping my mother make apple and rhubarb pie, clumsily chopping up Granny Smiths, when I had accidentally given myself a nasty cut on the thumb and run to the bathroom in search of a sticking plaster. There it was, propped up on the bottom shelf like some weird tribal offering. It sat next to a rusting blue razor. I took a plaster from the box, wrapped it round my cut thumb. Shut the door to the cabinet and returned to the kitchen for more chopping. I said nothing to anybody about what I had found. I didn't want to nark on my brother.

The skeleton was next. It hung suspended from the garage ceiling, unpolished, yellowing. It looked brittle. By this time, my mother was fairly resigned. Rather than berating her son about the strange objects, all now inanimate, all once animate, she chose to ignore the skeleton, the brain, the heart, to act as if nothing unusual was going on in our household. Being angry or upset, she reasoned, would only egg him on. Better to shrug it off, make another pot of fig jam, do a bit more cleaning, to act, most convincingly, as if she was not in the least disturbed by this odd accumulation of organs and bones that gathered about our home; this strange invasion.

My usual route home from school was along the Railway Reserve. This was an uninhabited stretch of land that, as the name would suggest, had been set aside in order that train tracks, running from the coast to our town, might one day be put there. The tracks had never been laid; they'd got some two hundred miles inland before deciding that supplies and passengers were better off hitting the road, but the reserve remained, like some weird reminder of all that could have been but never was. I liked the reserve, the long grass that reached up to my knees, the insects that hopped and buzzed about, the solitude. From a distance it looked like a cornfield. I was thirteen, on the verge of adolescence. I needed my time alone. Like my brother, I was an odd boy. *Different*, said my mother. But everybody knew what she meant. One of my favourite pastimes was throwing frogs against the garage wall and watching them splatter.

When I wasn't alone, I was often with my friend Vincent, who was considered unusual because of his flaming red hair. It took so little, to set you apart, to mark you out for ostracism. On my first day at high school, I'd saved Vincent from the impending fate of a 'dunny dunk' by giving one of the beefy fourth formers who held him a boot in the shins, and delivering a mean right hook to the nose of the other boy, who'd had the intended victim's arm pushed up behind his back. The previous summer, my brother had given me boxing lessons; he said I needed to know how to defend myself. He taught me how to make a fist, fingers tightly curled, thumb safely tucked in behind the knuckles. He taught me how to jab, how to dance lightly on my feet, how to feint. And about the forgotten arm. I didn't get angry often, but when I did, I was wild, like a pit bull on heat. There was nothing like mindless bullying to throw me into a rage. After I had punched and kicked and saved him, Vincent and I were bonded, tight. We pricked our fingers with a needle, rubbed them together, and swore to be blood brothers.

Although I liked Vincent's company, I sometimes needed to get away from him as well. He could be overbearing, clingy. At times I felt like he was smothering me. He would get jealous if I began forming friendships with other boys, would get in a huff and refuse to talk to me until I turned my attention, my efforts, back to him. This put me in a precarious position, as he was often sick with flu or migraine, and on those days, I was either forced to sit alone at lunch time and during breaks, or else, to try and approach some other group of boys, some clique, who always had their own rules, their own social codes, from which I was inevitably excluded. These days were torture and in order to make them more bearable, and to get some breathing space away from Vincent, I had begun to form a friendship with another boy, called Kyle. This union was based largely on a shared thrill gained from harming or destroying various creatures in the animal kingdom, from the great to the small. Kyle had a BB gun and a Swiss army knife that his uncle had given him for Christmas. The knife had a razor-sharp blade. We paralysed pigeons, maimed mice, crippled squirrels. One Sunday we took out the eye of an urban fox. Vincent was too soft for these games. He'd once started crying after I'd wounded the neighbour's cat with a slingshot. Kyle lived just around the corner from me; Vince's house was on the other side of town.

I loved wilderness; Vincent was a born suburbanite. One afternoon, he dragged me to see the new shopping mall that had just been constructed about a mile from our school.

"C'mon," he said. "They've got McDonalds in there and everything. I'll buy you a Big Mac."

I had never eaten McDonalds before and, because such food was forbidden in our household, it held a magical allure for me; the golden arches took on all the mystical grandeur of the gates of heaven itself. I didn't need much convincing. Vince and I walked silently, side by side, towards our destination.

When we arrived we made a beeline straight for McDonalds, and then headed for the centre of the mall where we leant nonchalantly against a wall, devouring our bounty. I was halfway through my burger when Vincent's arm shot out and pointed at a moving object in the near distance.

"Hey," he said, through a mouthful of Filet-O-Fish. "Check out the dumb guy in a bear suit."

Outside Toys R Us, to the tune of the Macarena, a bear danced alone. I knew exactly who it was in there, under all that fur, but I said nothing, just stared and continued stuffing my face. Nobody was paying David much attention; I assumed that either the mall or the toy store was employing him to entertain the after school crowds, but maybe I was wrong, maybe he was just amusing himself. Letting off steam. When the music finished he sat down on a nearby bench, removed the head of his suit and muttered to nobody in particular, "I used to want to be a doctor before I became a dancing bear."

Used to? I skulked back in the McDonalds doorway, terrified that he would see me and drag me into his pit of shame.

Vince nudged me hard in the ribs.

"Isn't that your brother?"

"Dunno. Don't think so. C'mon, let's get out of here."

I started walking away without him, knowing that he would follow.

I walked Vincent to his house, then doubled back on myself and meandered along the reserve for a while. This place had always felt like a sanctuary, now it felt desolate, empty, like a deserted children's playground. David had always wanted to be a doctor. As kids, I'd been his willing patient, stretching myself out on the kitchen table, pretending to be etherised while he prodded about, examining me, solemnly pronouncing tragic diagnoses. I never had more than days to live. I knew that he must've been kicked out of med school; I couldn't imagine him leaving voluntarily. Seeing him in his bear suit had disturbed me. Was this what adulthood had in store, this failure of dreams and ambition, this humiliation, this fall from grace?

That evening, I knocked on the door to David's room. When he didn't answer, I pushed open the door and entered anyway. He was lying on his bed, staring at the ceiling. I sat down on the end of his bed and picked at the bedspread, which was navy blue, covered in loops you could pull, unravel. The blades of the ceiling fan overhead spun slowly, softly, *whoosh, whoosh, whoosh.* Several books on alternative medicine graced his bookshelves.

"I saw you in the mall this afternoon," I said, after a spell.

"I know," he replied. "I saw you leaving."

There was a ten second pause that seemed as if it might open up and swallow us.

"I've been kicked out," he said eventually.

This time it was my turn to say, "I know."

"Wanna know why?"

"Of course."

His shoulders started shaking, though I was unsure whether this was with laughter, or some other emotion.

"Well, they have this head box, which is where they put the heads of cadavers after they've been severed from their bodies. Anyway, for a joke, I hooked up a mechanical laughing device, so that whenever you opened up the lid, you'd get this hideous cackling. Guess the dean of the school didn't see the funny side of it."

"Harsh."

"Yeah, everybody said how unfair it was."

Could you really be kicked out, just for that? Was he lying or telling the truth? Maybe he had done something else, something far worse. Maybe he had just got bored and quit.

"So what do you need those bits of bodies for now then?" I questioned. "All that stuff kind of creeps me out."

"Oh those. I've been nicking them. Don't tell Mum. She'd have a fit."

"Nicking them?"

"The dumb-arses forgot to take my swipe card back, so I've been sneaking past the security guard at night, getting into the labs and stealing shit. Whatever I can lay my hands on."

"But you've left now. You don't need that stuff anymore."

"I thought that maybe I could be, y'know, a self taught doctor."

"What? Don't be stupid. You need the training, the qualification. They'll take you back, Dave. They can't kick you out just for that."

"Oh, but they can though. They did. I don't care. In the meantime, I can earn some extra cash with the bear thing."

"Are you going to tell them?"

"Tell who?"

"Mum and Dad. You can't just keep pretending that you're still at med school forever."

"Yeah," he said. "One day. When I think they're ready."

He rolled over onto his stomach and turned his face into the pillow. I knew it was my cue to leave.

I trudged around to Kyle's house. We mucked about outside for a couple of hours, taunting the neighbour's Alsatian with a piece of steak on the end of a barbeque fork, dangling it over the fence, then yanking it back when he lunged for it, hosing down the cat with the water blaster that Kyle's dad had been using on the house, destroying every spider web we could find. When it grew too dark to see I told Kyle that it was time for me to go home.

"Hey," he said, as I was leaving. "I almost forgot what I was going to tell you. Yesterday morning I woke up early and I saw this bird, rare, you know, in the tree outside my window. Bright blue and yellow feathers. Looked like some kind of parrot."

"Wow," I said. "Weird. Maybe somebody's pet escaped."

"It was there again this morning, too. Like some kind of gaudy crow. Showing off, you know. Asking for it."

I laughed.

"Yeah. Show-off."

"So, anyway, if you get here tomorrow morning, early, before school, maybe we can get it with the BB gun. Just wound it. Stun it a little. Then we can examine it up close. Maybe it's never been seen before. Maybe we will have discovered a new species. You get money for that, you know. And fame."

He posed against the wall, a triumphant hunter, holding an imaginary bird by one scaly leg, hand on hip, chin at a jaunty angle.

"You're on," I said.

"Six-thirty."

"I'll set my alarm."

I awoke with the dawn, and made my way to my friend's house. One by one, the streetlights flickered off, as if the darkness was something contagious each lamp passed along to the next in line. Kyle was standing outside his house with his BB gun. As I approached he put his finger to his lips and pointed up at the shape in the tree. The bird looked enormous, out of place, a gigantic multi-coloured albatross. I had never seen anything like it in my life. Kyle took aim and fired. The pellet hit the bird squarely in the chest, right where its heart would be. It squawked once, then fell from the tree and landed with a solid thud at our feet.

"Holy shit," said Kyle. "It looks even bigger now. It's massive."

I was filled with a sudden panic.

"I think we've killed it. What if this bird's the last of its kind? Won't we get in trouble?"

"In trouble with who? Nobody's ever seen it except for you and me. Nobody else knows anything about it."

He plucked a feather from its plumage, and whistled long and low.

"Phew! Look at the size of that momma! Go on, Larry. Get plucking."

The bird looked so helpless, so defenceless, so dead. I felt nauseous, like I had been on a long, winding journey in the hot sun, in a car with all the windows wound up. But I couldn't risk Kyle thinking that I was soft, that I wasn't a man. I reached down and took two feathers, gave him the V-sign with them, then threw them scornfully to the ground. Not to be beaten, Kyle got to his knees and ripped two handfuls of plumage from the bird, laughed at me, or at something, and then stuffed the feathers down the front of his pants, like a codpiece. It was a competition now. I got down beside him and began pulling out great chunks of feathers, throwing them all around us, like the corny pillow ads I had seen on TV at other people's houses. The bird was still warm, like undercooked meat. Part of me wanted it to protest, to rise up against us, peck at our eyes and tear at our clothes, but it couldn't, of course, it couldn't. When we were done, we fell about laughing, keeling against one another like ships that had lost their ballast. The remains of the bird lay beneath the tree, plucked, like a chicken. When Kyle wasn't looking, I picked up a single blue feather and put it in my pocket.

The two of us walked to school and entered the classroom together, still laughing about the dumb bird. My right hand was in my pocket, wrapped around the quill of the feather. Vince was sitting by himself, arms folded, staring blankly into space. He was quiet for a moment, then got up from his chair and walked across to address Kyle.

"Did you know, *Mr Kyle,* that Larry's brother is a bear, a dancing bear."

Spit flew from his mouth as he pronounced the word *bear.*

"He's not a med student at all. He's a bear, a dumb *bear.*"

He began apeing about the classroom, humming the Macarena.

"Ehhhhhh Macarena."

Truth be told, I wasn't in the mood for it.

"Shut the fuck up, Vince." I said. "Shut the fuck up."

"Larry your family is *weird.* Rabbit food and no TV. No wonder you wound up *freaks.*"

"I'm telling you to shut your gob, you Mummy's boy, you faggot."

"Faggot? Who're you calling faggot, Kyle lover. Kyle, wanna come kill some pigeons? Kyle, wanna rip the hind legs off a cat?"

Something exploded near the front of my head. I lunged at him, grabbed him by the collar and shoved him against the wall.

"Shut your fucking face, or I'll shut it for you."

"Kyle wanna come suck my cock?"

That was when I left him have it, socked him one, full in the face. His head hit the wall behind him with a thwack, and then he slumped down on the ground, out cold. Out for the count. His nose hung crooked, broken, on his face. I was sent to the headmaster's office. Severely reprimanded. Threatened with suspension and given three detentions.

At home, something else had been broken; the news. My mother was furious. She'd gathered up all David's medical textbooks, the heart, the brain, the bones and thrown the lot out onto the street. She'd kicked my brother out also, shoved him through the door and told him to go and get himself a proper job, and somewhere else to live, she wasn't going to pay for his food, his clothes, his electricity, if he wasn't going to toe the line. He'd been caught sneaking into the department at night. The school dean had rung her up and told her the whole sorry story.

"And the *worst* part is," she was yelling, as I turned into the driveway, "the very worst part is that you lied to me. You deceived me. Pretending to be a part-time bear, when really you were full-time and had nothing else to do, nowhere else to go."

When David saw me, he just shrugged his shoulders, plucked a pair of jeans and a T-shirt from his belongings that were out on the street, gave us all a small wave and trudged off into the distance. God only knew where he was going.

That night I dreamt that the bird was at my window, featherless. You could see its skeleton through its skin.

"I'm sorry," I said. "I'm sorry."

But the bird just shook its head sorrowfully from side to side and tears like blue jewels fell from its eyes. And I knew that what had been done was done, and could never be undone or forgotten.

# THE MAN WHO WANTED A BABY

They were everywhere. They were always everywhere, inescapable, like vermin. They came in all shapes and sizes, and in a variety of colours; white, black, brown, yellow, red and pink and squealing. They got in the parks, both out in the open and back lurking behind the trees, small murderers waiting to pounce. They infested the swimming pools, the trains, the supermarkets, the buses, the airports. They were full of demands, impossible demands; ice-creams, lollies, Teletubbies, Eminem action dolls. They wanted monkeys and lions and bears. They were a need that could never be satisfied, a hole that could never be filled. Their mouths gaped open to reveal an empty sea of wanting, an unquenchable thirst, a hunger that made her recoil in fear of its intensity. She blanked them out as best she could; hummed to herself, made mental lists of tasks she had to do the next day, rewrote old song lyrics in her head, twisting and turning the words and their meaning. But no matter how she tried they were always there. Snotty noses. Pissed-in pants.

Speaking of things that were always there. She turned the key in the lock and pushed open the door to see him on the sofa, (*surprise!* he was *always* on the damned sofa), Ruthie cradled in his lap, an enormous spliff in his right hand, the remote beside him and an open can of beer upon the coffee table. On this, as on many other occasions, she found the words *Don't you have a home to go to?* forming, almost involuntarily in her mind, before remembering that this *was* his home. He had nowhere else to go. They continued to go through the motions, though the emotion had long since departed.

He looked up at her, pouting.

"You're late," he said.

She shrugged, waiting for the Spanish inquisition. *Where have you been, who have you been with, what were you doing*, each second of your life accountable, marked down, the columns tallied up like debits and credits. *Do you balance?* Today he chose a different tack; he decided to play on her guilt.

"Ruthie needs feeding."

"Well feed her then," she snapped, dumping down her handbag and heading into the kitchen for a glass of white wine.

Placing the joint in the ashtray, he switched off the telly and followed on her heels, holding Ruth up over his shoulder, face downwards, in a perfect position to puke all down his back. He stood in the doorway as she uncorked the wine and sighed, a deep, long sigh, like a man put upon, as if *she* was the one making demands on *him*. As soon as her wine was poured (but before she'd had a chance to drink any of it) he pushed the small package (head, torso, limbs) into her arms, where it lay as still as a dead thing. He began the preparation of heating the milk, putting it into the bottle, testing it ever so carefully on his wrist, pausing every now and then to look at her beseechingly. She felt like kicking him. Instead, she simply opened her arms and let Ruth fall to the ground, where she landed on the hard tiled floor of the kitchen with a thud. Then she picked her glass of wine took a long swig and stomped up the stairs to the bedroom, oblivious to his cries of horror.

In the corner of the bedroom sat a stack of small nappies, all neatly folded, ready to be wrapped and pinned upon Ruthie's tiny bottom. She kicked this pile over and plonked down upon the futon, spilling white wine over herself as she did so, cursing as she kicked off her shoes. She picked up the stereo remote and cranked the volume up to eight. She heard his foot upon the stair, and turned up the volume still further, as if she could simply drown him out. The ashtray on top of the stereo started to rattle and shake. He stood reproachfully in the doorway.

Sometimes she felt that she could predict his every move, his every word, his every breath. Flicking through the catalogue of her own emotions, she found that she felt nothing; no guilt, no pity, no remorse. She wished she had a wand to vanish him, to melt him into a puddle, or to turn him into stone right where he stood.

"Well?" he said.

"Well what?"

"She's cracked," he croaked, choking slightly on the words, before turning Ruthie over and holding her aloft in order to force her to see the damage that she'd done.

It was true. The plastic head had split open at the back and when you did as he was doing now (pushing inwards on both her ears simultaneously) the cranium split open to reveal the hollow inside.

"Well chuck her back in the study and get another one then," she said. "She's hardly indispensable."

He frowned, an illogical man searching for a logical argument. Then, for want of anything good to say, he muttered *You're inhuman,* under his breath, before turning his back on her, picking up a nappy and a safety pin and traipsing off down the stairs to go about this fictional business of 'taking care of Ruthie.' Later he'd be in wanting sex, wanting to *procreate,* while she lay there bored, staring at the ceiling. Sometimes she felt that he was something she'd programmed herself during a lengthy fit of masochism.

In order that she could hear what was happening on the floor below, she turned down the volume on the stereo and, when she heard the telly being switched on, she rose up off the bed and went through into the room which had once been her study but was now given over to the accommodation of Ruthies, a whole *room* full of them, a shipment, a gaggle, a *fleet*; Ruthies sucking their thumbs, Ruthies asleep, awake, sitting, crawling and standing; all the same make and model – brown hair, blue eyes. Little plastic clones that all said *Mama* when you pushed their middles. A hole for the mouth, to take in fluid, and a hole at the other end to piss it out. *Mamamamamama.* He liked to go in there at the weekend, when he was bored and press all their tummies willy-nilly, sparking off a riot of mechanical voices, a flat demanding chorus that sounded to her ears like *moremoremoremoremoremore.* She surveyed the collection with disdain.

She locked the door to the study with the bolt she'd had fitted with the specific purpose of shutting him out and then shunted aside a few members of this horrid clan in order to make some room in which to test the special unit. She'd tested every function a hundred times already, but lost in the woods it can get hard to see the trees and she needed to run through everything one last time. In the beginning she'd desired perfection, but now, at the end, she had settled for functionality. She was running out of time; she needed to escape, to get back to the other place before she blew a fuse. *Beware of geeks bearing gifts,* she thought to herself as she placed her marvellous toy upon the table. She logged on and ran through the basic commands; tested the response times. When to cry, when to crawl, when to sleep, when to smile – though she tested them now though keystrokes, when she was gone the two-way transmission/reception system would ensure that voice commands could be transmitted via a cellular telephone network. Upon receiving a message, the software then executed commands that the custom built operating system converted into ones and zeroes – communication at a level the circuitry could understand. An absence and then a presence. Something and then nothing. A similar two-way system installed in the unit sent messages notifying its state back to the sender. Signals flying back and forth through space. The controller code was on their site: inaccessible except to those who were in the know. This was, in part, a preventative measure against untimely self-expiration. No matter what became of her, they would know what to do. She was part of a larger plan. There was a clock in its chest to simulate heartbeat.

It was well within her intellectual means to develop the software and the operating system; the hardware had been a different question. She had done a decent job with everything except the skin and the eyes. The skin *looked* ok, it just didn't feel right, too rubbery, too sticky to the touch and no matter how vigilantly she powered it with talc it still *smelt* strange. The eyes were too glassy, too inanimate, and although they swung on pivots, giving them a good up, down and left to right range, any fool staring into those peepers for more than five seconds would be sure to understand that he looked not at a thing born, but at something made. It wouldn't matter if he knew that this thing did not live; she had ensured that he had become accustomed to automata, expected it, in fact, thought it harmless. Impossible to tell how many others would be fooled. This was a long term plan, not something that could be executed overnight. All over the city, others were doing as she was, creating simulacra; enemies disguised as friends. She would not let the side down. She would play her part; she would see it through.

The first time that she picked it up she'd had a big surprise. It had not lain still, but instead, had kicked soundlessly in her arms, legs thrashing wildly, like a possessed wind-up toy. She did not believe in demons. She'd talked logic to herself. Everything has a reason. Cause precedes effect. She'd looked around the room and discovered that she'd accidentally knocked a book onto the keyboard, inadvertently causing continuous pressing of the 'leg thrash' key combination and thereby creating the disturbance. With relief at having found the source of the animation, she had removed the book from the keyboard and, with a strange whirring sound, the unit had grown suddenly still. That single incident aside, the entire operation had run very smoothly and she could confirm that the product was now ready. It was a neat unit, tidy. Form followed function. It obeyed every command that it was sent and none that it was not.

Satisfied that all was in order and that she could proceed, she sent an email to the others, and left the study for the bedroom. He was in there, on the futon. He said nothing. When she lay down, still in the pin-striped suit she had been wearing all day, he simply took her knickers off, inserted himself like a coin into a slot machine, and started pumping away. She stared at a spider that had, for several weeks, been spinning a gossamer web in one corner of the ceiling. In a matter of minutes he had finished, rolled over and was snoring. His favourite Ruthie lay beside their futon in a small basket, her eyes pressed closed, on her side, in the recovery position, a small plastic Moses; a clone. She was far too wired to sleep. She quietly crept from the room.

She took the chosen unit from the study and carried it downstairs to the lounge, where she arranged it neatly amongst the sofa cushions. A still imitation of life. Its mouth was smiling and its eyes looked kind. It stared straight ahead at his favourite household God, the television. Its benign appearance hid her murderous intent.

Christ, she was exhausted. She stripped out of her suit, wiped off her makeup with a damp tissue and some cleanser, shook out her hair and rolled her neck from side to side in an effort to unwind.

She peeled back her own skin, pulled some wires, disconnected.

# SPROUT

By anybody's standards it was an expensive duvet. It was the best, a leader, a king amongst quilts. It was different from the rest. It was the fluffiest, the warmest, the finest. Fifty percent down and fifty percent large feather, it was not dressed up to the nines, like many of the others, the show-offs, in their gaudy coloured prints and their florals and their tartan covers. It was plain, naked, but it shone with potential. Once inside the cover he had designed, it would knock the competition into a cocked hat. It was a diamond in the rough.

They had come here together to find it. Hand in hand at Benny's For Beds on a Sunday, they'd walked down the duvet aisle, testing and fluffing and plumping, shaking their heads in dismay as candidate after candidate had failed to measure up. And now, just as they had begun to give up hope, here it was, sitting quietly on its own, slightly apart from the others, like a shy pet waiting to be chosen from amongst all the others in the store, overlooked because it didn't bark or turn back flips.

She had a feeling about it. She just knew. Goose bumps on her arms, a shiver down her spine. A strong sense of recognition gripped her, as if she had seen this duvet somewhere before, known it, perhaps intimately, in some other place, in some other life. It was the last one of its kind left on the shelf. She clutched it to her chest like a Linus blanket and gave him *the look*, the look which said *we've found it*. He shrugged, knowing that she was right, averting his eyes from the plastic pricing label tacked to the front of the shelf it had been on. Two small white feathers floated slowly to the ground.

It wasn't cheap. Three day's salary gone in an instant, on a plain cotton cover and some plucked plumage. She shrugged off the expense. It was worth it. It would cover her.

She carried it to the checkout with him trailing just behind, lost in his own little world. She watched protectively as the cashier rang up the purchase and placed her new charge in a large plastic carry bag. She smiled as she handed across her Visa, smiled as they walked across the car park, smiled all the way home, nestled already with her head upon its warmth, smiled as they took it inside, up the stairs where they snuggled together sleepily for a while before falling asleep beneath its cosy warmth. When they awoke it was night time and the room was filled with a strange light. Groggily, she propped herself up on one elbow and peered through the pane, expecting that perhaps the moon was full tonight, or a few extra stars shone, or the council had erected an extra street lamp outside their house. Nothing outside was shining. The night was dark and cloudy, with a soft rain falling.

He raised himself up beside her, one arm around her waist. "It's this thing," he said, patting their latest acquisition tentatively. "It's glowing."

Disbelieving, she looked down, and saw that although more a feeble glimmer than a brilliant radiation, the thing was, unmistakably, emitting a dull glow. Its light shone out between the dark seagull shapes he'd designed for its handmade, screen-printed cover.

"Spooky," he whispered, awed.

She picked up one corner of the thing that covered them and fluffed it about, as if the incandescence could be shaken out, as if she suspected that perhaps somebody had planted a few of those awful glow sticks in there amongst the feathers for a joke. Or something electronic and cellular that could be switched on from a distance.

"Maybe it's genetically engineered," he said. "Like those fish with the phosphorescent jellyfish genes."

She laughed, as you would laugh at a child who had discovered some awful truth that, for their own protection, they would have been better off not knowing. Thinking that perhaps to irradiate it with some greater light would stun it into behaving appropriately, she switched on the bedside lamp. Her hunch was right. The duvet flickered, faded and died.

It was not to glow again for several weeks.

There was a more pressing problem with the duvet. It moulted. It had a plumage retention issue. Further, rather than merely confining themselves to the boudoir, the freed feathers saw fit to migrate, and would drift insidiously down the stairs to lodge themselves in strange places. Feathers were found prettily displayed amongst a bouquet of blooms in the living room, neatly curled around a lemon in the fruit bowl, spiked into a pound of butter which had been stored in the door of the fridge. "How come they're never just on the floor," he asked, when the freed feather fiasco first started. "Why do they always have to *show off?*"

She felt the need to defend the duvet and its offspring.

"They're not doing it on purpose," she said. "It's just coincidence that they come to rest in such strange places."

"It's like they're trying to spite us," he muttered, before going back to picking a scab that had formed on his elbow as a result of a scrape he'd incurred while renovating the bathroom. That was the first sign of resentment he showed towards her precious purchase.

She always found herself taking its side. He wanted to take it back to the store. He thought it was possessed; a demon duvet.

"I wish I'd never made that damned cover," he said. "Then none of this would have happened."

"O don't be so ridiculous," she scoffed, faintly amused by such neurotic notions. "It's as warm as toast. And besides, it's happy here."

He looked at her sideways.

"Happy? How the hell can a duvet be *happy?* You think the little fucker has *feelings?*"

She'd shrugged.

"You know what I mean. It's full and fluffy."

"And that in itself is unnatural," he had countered. "How can it lose so many feathers and still be *fluffy?*"

"It's special," she said. "It's not like the others."

She felt like she was sticking up for some prodigious, bratty child.

"No good can come of it," he muttered and turned his back on her.

She was siding with the enemy; he felt ganged up upon, ostracized in his own home. He formed his own team of one. She heard him banging about in his studio, slapping down paint and kicking in canvases and cursing. She knew not what he was making.

The cupboards that lined the walls of his studio were filled with his creations. In the early days, he'd painted only her, from the side, from the front, from the rear. Nudes, mostly. When they'd lived in different cities she'd flown up to see him one weekend and flown back with one of his versions of herself tucked under her arm. The stewardess had made her put the painting in the overhead locker and something had fallen on it, crushing her right buttock, so that it looked like she'd had a bad dose of liposuction. She'd been his subject for six months and then she had grown tired of posing for him; she told him that he needed new material. As if out of spite, he had started painting other women instead. Bank tellers, mutual friends, a thirteen year old girl he'd paid five bucks to take off her clothes so he could render her immortal. He thought he was doing her a favour.

But she was what he kept returning to. She was the default. Although she had stopped posing for him, he had not stopped attempting to render her in paint. He didn't show his work to anyone, not even her. She was forbidden from his study. Occasionally she would rescue a painting from the garbage and get a glimpse of his interior world. Once, after a fight, he'd painted her as a six headed monster, holding him up in a massive claw, mouth open, ready to devour. In another he had shown her giving a faceless man a blow job in a seedy bar. He signed and dated nothing. These pictures could have been made by anybody. Or nobody at all.

They'd had the thing for just over three weeks when he noticed the first sprout. They were lying in bed together and she was (in retrospect somewhat foolishly) lying on her side, facing away from him, when he reached out a hand and prodded her in the middle of her back.

"There's something weird here. Near your spine. Like a pimple only bigger."

She attempted to roll over onto her back so he couldn't see it, but he propped a hand under her shoulder and hoisted her over, pressing his face up close to her skin.

"Christ," he said. "It's massive. Here, let me squeeze."
After picking, squeezing was his favourite activity. He sat up straight and crouched over her. Craning her neck she could see his brow furrowed in concentration as he placed an index finger on either side of the offending lump and pushed. Nothing. He pushed again, harder, and then gasped, as if some kindly aunt never before prone to violence had just slapped him across the face.

"What?" She questioned innocently. "What is it?"
She knew damned well what it was. Or what it might be.
"It's this *thing*," he said descriptively. "Protruding. Like a weird white stick."
She didn't want to appear too defensive.
"Just leave it alone," she said. "I'll go to the doctor and get it checked out. I had a mole removed there a couple of years before I met you. Maybe it's just... you know. Old mole bits gone funny."
"Hang on," he said. "I think I can yank it out. Where's your tweezers?"
"Don't yank it," she said. "You'll only make it bleed."
She pointed to his weeping elbow as evidence of the evils of picking and yanking.
"It'll be fine," he said, rising to his feet and fossicking about on the dresser. "Just hold still."
Before she could protest he had gripped the thing in the claws of the tweezers and, in one swift movement, like removing a sticking plaster, hauled it out.
"Holy shit," he said, holding the removed object up to the light. "It's over an inch long."
"Maybe it's a thorn," she said, grasping at straws.
Too slender.
He held the thing he had plucked between forefinger and thumb and snapped it neatly in two.
"Brittle," he said accusatorily, and gave her a cold look, as if he had fallen asleep one night next to one person and awoken the next morning next to somebody else entirely.
"It's nothing," she said. "Don't worry about it."
Although they shared most things, there are always secrets that each individual must keep private, even from those closest to

them, and these shoots, these *sprouts*, as she had named them in her mind, were something that she had preferred to keep to herself.

She left the room and plodded downstairs to the bathroom. In the shower she applied hair removal cream to her entire body. It was a precaution she took in between the bouts of electrolysis, which for everybody else was permanent, but which, for her, was only a temporary solution. She was spending a fortune and she dreaded the sessions. The electrolysist was beginning to ask questions. She put another red rinse through her hair, stepped out of the steam and dried herself. Her body was covered in small tender red bumps, not unlike the measles. She looked in the mirror and breathed a sigh of relief. Her face, as yet had been spared.

One evening she returned home from work to find him in the lounge, standing above the duvet and beating it with the wooden spoon that she used to stir soups and casseroles.
"What the...?"
He stopped suddenly and swung round to face her. Fire was in his eyes.
"It spat at me," he said, and reached out his right hand to give the thing another whack.
"It spat?"
"*Poisonous* spit," he added, "Venom. Look."
And he pulled down the collar of his shirt to reveal a great red welt that swelled purple around the edges.
"What the hell is *that*?"
"*That* was caused by *this*," he said, and took down from the mantelpiece a jar which contained a single button, a button which she recognized as having come from the cover of the duvet. She noticed that the lid of the jar was firmly on, with breather holes punched through it, as if the button was some rare biological specimen that he had captured.
"Are you trying to tell me that a single tiny button caused that enormous welt?"
"Oh, this ain't no ordinary button," he said. "The little bugger's infused its buttons with *venom*."

"But the cover's separate," she said. "The cover's nothing to do with it."

"It has *become* its cover," he said theatrically, before throwing the wooden spoon down in disgust and stomping upstairs to nurse his wound.

And the poor thing lay in the corner, quivering from the beating it had taken, shaking like a jelly in an earthquake. She picked up the jar that contained the small blue button, and held it up to the light. So small, so harmless! Was it possible that he had cut himself on purpose, set the duvet up, framed it? Or incurred the wound in some other manner, and thought afterwards to blame it on the duvet? She didn't know whom to trust anymore. She found it hard to believe that the duvet had lashed out unprovoked. Even in the unlikely event that he *was* telling the truth and the button *had* been fired at will, he must have done something to cause it to act in such a violent manner. She put down the jar, picked up the duvet and snuggled on the sofa, not wanting to venture upstairs and disrupt the wounded one. It was the first night they had spent apart in three years.

Over the following weeks the duvet became a thing ineffable. To speak of it was to widen the divide between them even further, to do anything other than ignore it was to make the air too thick for even the sharpest knife to slice through. The tension of not mentioning was killing her. Upon entering their formerly happy home, at the end of her day, she felt herself grow pale, felt the blood draining from her body, as if leeched by some invisible vampire. She found herself looking into mirrors in strange rooms at strange times, as if she would see something behind her, something that lurked just beyond her right shoulder, a sinister Spirit of Resentments Past. A thing unbottled. She knew he could feel it too. Never a loquacious man, he now became even more sullen, silent and withdrawn, like a teenager. He had fenced off parts of himself, erected Keep Out signs. Large areas were off limits. He was a closed book. His paintings turned black; he had entered his noir phase. His work became a dark room that could not be lit. Before he had kept them hidden, now he left them round the house for her to see, these renderings of dead birds and spiders and rats.

Others were noticing the strain of these changes. Kathleen from the office took her out to lunch and, in between the Caesar salads and the coffee, asked if everything was alright. "Things are slipping," Kathleen said. "Standards. We all have our off days, but an agenda for a meeting was sent out with the wrong address, resulting in several senior managers lost in cabs in the vicinity of Fleet Street when they were needed in the inner city. They're busy people. They need accuracy from their support staff. They need you to be present in both body and mind."
Pause. Sip of cappuccino.
"We're not indispensable you know."
Razor-edged words bound up in cotton wool. In response, she smiled and sipped her coffee, pulling her shirt cuffs down to hide her wrists.
"Mind on the job, please," Kathleen continued, flashing her pearly whites like a small shark that has smelt blood. "And if you want to talk, I'm always here."
It was then that Kathleen reached out to pat her knee, before jerking back in alarm. She had hit bristles, stumps.
"Spanish genes," she said eventually, after a long, pregnant pause, and shrugged, her fair hair and pale skin illuminating the lie. "A bit of a curse."
They were poking out through her stockings now. She'd missed an electrolysis appointment last week and had not been plucking. She smiled, paid the bill, and went back to the office a model of efficiency, a secretarial robot, typing and filing and answering the phone like a thing programmed. Every now and then she would stop and run her right hand along her left arm, from the wrist towards the elbow, feel how strange it felt, like stroking velvet against the grain. Then she would run her hand back the other way, smoothing ruffled feathers.

Every day she sprouted a little more, sprouted painfully and unfairly. Every day he said nothing. He had given up, was pretending not to notice. She began skipping work, calling in two or three times a week to say she couldn't come in that day, lying around the house, giving the odd desultory pluck. Fighting a losing battle. She pleaded illness, family crisis, dental appointments, death. She kept a list of relatives whose funerals she'd already given as excuses for not making it in, so that she never gave the same name twice. On the days she did go in, she baked, boiled beneath her long trousers and shirts and feathers. It was like wearing a sleeping bag underneath her clothes. She saw the other girls giving her glances. Kathleen had been talking. Cruelly, somebody printed out a copy of *Metamorphosis* and left it on her desk for her to find.

She thought he might say something, comment, call a doctor. Instead, he simply spent increasing amounts of time away from the house and down at the pub, coming home and passing out on the sofa, where she would inevitably find him the next morning, snoring in a pile of his own puke. When he wasn't drunk he was working, holed up in his studio, producing yet more pictures of creatures that crept or crawled or flew by night. The bat phase she found particularly disturbing, entailing as it did, his endless visits to the zoo, where he would lurk in the nocturnal enclosure for hours, frightening small children with the sketchings of vampires that he would give away for free.

One night he didn't come home at all, didn't call from the pub to stay he would be late, didn't stagger home in the early morning hours, bleary and apologetic. He became now simply an absence. He became something missing.

That same night, at four in the morning, as she had snuggled deeper into its warmth, the duvet had begun to glow. This time she didn't try and stop it, didn't put it in its place, didn't switch on the overhead light in order to dazzle it into submission. This time the light seemed not sinister, but friendly, comforting. She had settled down into its light, bathed in its warmth, as if wallowing in a sun-kissed ocean, floating beneath small golden stars. It had thrown its corners around her and together they had spent a wonderful night, slipping in and out of sleep and caresses. She remembered thinking that she had never felt so loved, so adored, so cherished.

He was there when she awoke, standing at the foot of the bed and looking down at her in disgust.

When she looked down at her arms, she could no longer see the skin beneath the feathers.

"Of all the people"…. he began, and then stopped, choking.

She was coated from shoulder to wrist with plumage, with the odd stray tuft of white down sprouting from the backs of her hands. Still struggling to wake, she rose groggily to her feet and stood in her underwear before the full length mirror. The duvet lurked guiltily upon the bed. Complicit.

"I just never thought you'd…"

He couldn't carry on. She had been claimed, taken over. Invaded. It wasn't just her arms; it was her legs, her stomach, her back, her bum, everything white with the odd grey speckle. Nothing on the face, Jehovah be praised, nothing on the face. She could smell the alcohol on his breath.

"…betray me like this. Look at yourself, just look!"

She did look. She saw.

"I can't stand it!" He screamed. "You can't even see what's happening to you. I'm leaving. I'm leaving you to it."

She shrugged. Nothing was sinking in; everything was bouncing off the surface. Water off a duck's back.

"That's it? That's all I get? A shrug? Seven years of my life and you brush it off with a shrug? The love of my life starts turning into a fucking *chicken* and all I get is a shrug?"

The dam gates had burst; he was a man in full flood.

"You start an affair with a duvet, a fucking *quilt* that I willingly allowed into our home and you expect me to just stand by and watch you being taken from me? Spirited away? I can't stand it. I am *OUT OF HERE*!!"

He fumbled briefly, drunkenly, in the wardrobe, shoved whatever pithy bounty he had retrieved into a small backpack, lurched down the stairs, slammed the front door and was gone.

She couldn't go to work; she couldn't go anywhere. She reached for her mobile and left a message for Kathleen.

"Can't come in. Won't be in for a while. Sorry."

Then she sunk back onto the bed and it wrapped its left, and then its right hand side around her.

She went out at first. Braved life as a feathered thing. Attempted to adjust to life's strange changes. When she went to the pub, she wore long trousers and a polo neck, left her gloves on as she clutched her pint of beer. The only parties she attended were fancy dress, where she strapped on a beak and went as a chicken, or a goose or some other kind of flightless fowl.

"Love your costume," people would coo. "God, so realistic. Where on earth did you get it?"

"Overseas," she would say, offhand, noncommittal. "In some other country."

Men found themselves inexplicably attracted to her soft covering, would want to stroke and pluck and pull.

"Jesus, these look and feel so real."

And they would turn to her, the expression upon their faces a strange mixture of wonderment and repulsion. It never went further than that. She was not the kind of girl that you could take home to mother.

She got by. There was one terrible incident at the supermarket in which she forgot to keep her gloves on, grew hot and pulled them off absent-mindedly, an incident in which some stupid young checkout chick mistook her feathered right hand for some strange unclassified product from the poultry section and passed it over the scanner. When the hand did not bleep, the checkout girl looked down and saw what she was holding, then started screaming hysterically. Seeing the manager heading towards her, she dropped her groceries and sprinted from the store, ran all the way home, heart beating double time. She cowered beneath her beloved cover and did not leave her room for a week. When she finally did emerge, she took to ordering her groceries online.

The duvet had its own mind. When it grew grey at the edges she attempted to wash it, but the damned thing stubbornly resisted, slithering from the steel interior of the front loader every time she tried to shove it in. In the end she threw her hands up, *okay you win. Be grubby. See if I care.* And to herself she thought, *the battle but not the war.* She snuck up on it one morning as it dozed, lying like a cat in the sun, dragged it into the laundry and turned on the taps. It reared up like a horse and whacked her in the face with a fore corner. She slapped it back, pushed it down in the tub and gave it another good dousing, then shut the door and left it in there to soak. When she returned half an hour later, it lay there dormant, as if all the life had been rinsed out of it. She wrung it with her hands and hung it out to dry. When she brought it back inside it sulked for a week, wouldn't glow, wouldn't snuggle. It would turn itself freezing cold in the middle of the night, so that she would awake shivering. Her feathers started to fall out, leaving small white scars from the places where they had grown. Eventually she gave in and apologized and promised never to wash it again. It acquiesced, but a rift had been created. She was driving everything away.

He still had his keys. She hadn't changed the locks. She could have sworn that he was entering the house when she was gone, sneaking in while she was out. She stood outside his study. This Pandora pushed open the door.

This had always been his private room, his space away from her, and now that he had left she went through his belongings with curiosity, looking for something, some letter, some diary, something that would in some way incriminate him. She ventured into forbidden places – the cupboards.

She began at the beginning, with the pictures of herself seven years ago, poised and smiling, a target of somebody else's imagination. He'd been into bright primaries at the time and she had been rendered in violently bright shades; her eyes like cornflowers, her lips glowing red, her mouth open, like an invitation. Her skin jaundice yellow. Later, with the bank tellers and the thirteen year old, he'd turned to fleshier tones; dusky pink and beige, shades of muted orange. It was like looking through a photograph album; snapshots that his mind had taken. She found the design for the material from which the duvet's cover was made; little seagulls flying across an endless ocean. More pictures of birds. Hawks and vultures and gulls. Birds exotic and extinct; macaws and moas and dodos. On his desk, a copy of *The New Encyclopedia of Birds*. Turning to the relevant pages, she could see that he'd adapted the drawings from this book, enlarged, envisioned, coloured them in. And then the hybrids. Men with sharp claws and beady-eyed women with beaks. Paintings which grew increasingly outlandish, featuring characters which looked like extras from *Alice In Wonderland.* Pictures, which, when put together, told a tale, a story book, something sinister and not for children. She sat down on the floor, surrounded by these things which had been made by her Brother Grim. Pictures of herself with beak and claws. Her own self as winged thing. Some strange voodoo.

Something was tearing at the inside of her skin. Something inside wanted out. She was bursting, transforming, becoming something other. She saw sideways now, and not straight ahead. The world had become peripheral. She beat one wing against the window, dug her talons into the sill.

In another part of the city, he smiled to himself, removed his jacket, relaxed.

"So," he said, leaning closer to the redhead at the bar. "You don't have a fear of flying, do you?"

## THE MOST ORDINARY MAN IN THE WORLD

Ordinarily, my sister would have packed just the five bikinis for our annual trip to the Costa del Sol, but, as she patiently explained to me in the car on the way to the airport, she wasn't getting any younger, and if she wanted to find a husband before she turned forty, she needed to start getting savvy and part of getting savvy was never being seen twice in the same bikini. Seven days meant seven different bikinis; all of which were suitably skimpy and glamorous. She'd been under a sun bed every day for the last month, ignoring my protests that it wasn't healthy, that she'd give herself cancer, that her skin would turn to leather. She'd peroxided every last shred of colour out of her hair and wore her makeup thick like camouflage paint. War paint. She was going into battle. She looked awful, but I reassured her that she looked terrific. She seemed man-made.

On the plane, she drank Evian water and turned away the in-flight meal in favour of the small sticks of carrot and celery she'd brought with her. I dutifully ate the pasta and pudding that sat upon the small plastic tray, then ordered a whisky and soda. When my drink arrived, Felicity frowned and said 'I didn't know you drank hard liquor.' Halfway through the flight, someone in first class started calling 'Felicity, Felicity'. (Nobody ever shortened her name - she was definitely not a 'Flick'). Felicity went to investigate and found it was somebody she knew from 'the industry' who had a spare seat next to them, being as an assistant had pulled out at the last minute. She came back for her handbag and said she knew I wouldn't mind if she sat up there for the flight. I smiled and nodded and sipped my whisky, watching her small frame, encased in its tight black dress, slide smoothly down the aisle, as if she had wheels attached to her feet.

"I'd like to introduce you to my brother – the most ordinary man in the world," she used to say, before she stopped inviting me to her exhibition openings.
I was commonplace, I was average. I was the median; the mid point from which all other men deviated. She hesitated to use the world dull. My invites (*'Felicity Farnsworth – 15 years in*

*Fashion Photography'* ) had stopped arriving after a woman had fallen asleep standing up when I had been talking amiably to her about databases. I had just finished explaining indexes and foreign key constraints, and was moving onto views and inner joins, when Felicity approached and pointed out, less than tactfully, that my 'victim's' eyes were closed and that she was dribbling and swaying dangerously to one side, as if about to fall into the table holding the hors d'oeuvres. It was an effect I often had on others and I'd learnt not to let it bother me. I told myself that the semi-conscious mind is able to absorb information more deeply than a mind that is fully awake. I fantasised about this when standing before my rows of dozing students; that their somnambulant state was osmotic, that the information I divulged was sinking in deeper and deeper, to some inner chamber of the brain, to the central processing unit, where it would be digested appropriately, mused upon, advanced to a higher level and spat back at me in tests and assignments and end-of-year exams in the form of crystallized genius. The evidence would suggest that my Theorem of Osmotic Learning was fatally flawed, for at the end of every year it was noted by the Head of Department that one third of the students had dropped out of my course, another third had failed outright and the victorious remainder had straggled in with Bs and Cs. Leaving the department was not a consideration; it was my safety haven. I was not a man who liked to venture into the unknown. I was not a tightrope walker. I liked both feet on the ground.

When she first called me ordinary I misheard her. What I thought she'd said was *I'd like to introduce you to my brother – the most lonely man in the world.* And maybe she had said that, though she denied it when I, atypically, confronted her about it afterwards.

"Ordinary," she said. "It's not an *insult.* Why do you always have to take these things the wrong way?"

And then she quickly turned her face in the opposite direction. Somewhere nearby a camera was clicking and she was keen to be caught on film.

The holiday rules had not changed since she had first dictated them ten years ago. I was not to do anything that would put other men off approaching her. I was not to lie next to her on the beach. I was not to talk to her without first giving the agreed signal and waiting for that signal's reply. If the reply was negative, I was not to approach. She didn't want me ruining her chances.

"If I'm such a liability, then why do you bother to bring me along?" I asked, the third time we took such a trip together. "You need it," she said. "If it wasn't for me, you'd barely leave your little office. All work and no play. Also, I promised Mother, just before she died, that I would take care of you." Misguided loyalty. Duty and guilt. Sisterly love.

One year I stayed at home, and Felicity went alone. "Fine," she huffed, as I broke the news that I intended to spend my summer leave holed up with my new computer. "You only cramp my style anyway." She came home filled with tales of the dashing Italian she had met, but I didn't see photos of anything other than the same old beach she always lay upon. She said she would be flying out to Rome to meet him, but there was no trip to Italy, and the next year she bought me the plane ticket six months in advance and stated that she wouldn't take no for an answer. She knew what was good for me.

As usual, I was staying in the youth hostel. It was something my sister suggested the first year of our trip, thinking it would help me to 'meet people'. It had the opposite effect. In August, the hostel was swarming with humans, most of them less than half my age. They filled up the dorms and the bathrooms and the kitchen with their noises and their clutter and their pointless babbling. This year, I'd treated myself to a private room, having suffered over-hearing the mating grunts and wise-cracking comments of a teenage couple in a mixed dorm the previous season. Away from my departmental hideaway, I was a fish out of water. I felt exposed, vulnerable, a crustacean without its crust. In the dormitories, I had nothing to hide behind, no walls with which to keep the inside in and the outside out. I was out in the open. Such feelings forced me to retreat inwards, to the point where, in my final year of dormitory dwelling, I'd overheard one smart-arse referring to me as 'that weird ageing mute on the top bunk'. This remark, along with the huffs and puffs and groans which had come from the bunk below later on that same evening, had assisted me in making up my mind that the following year I would reach a little deeper into my wallet and shell out for a private room.

Felicity was staying down the road in the five star 'Pearl of the Costa'; an ostentatious affair with gilded banisters, three swimming pools and large private suites, each of which had its own spacious balcony. Every now and then I would go up to her room for a drink, but mostly I just stood outside each morning, waiting to escort her to the beach. She didn't like to walk to the sea alone.

"There he is, my big brave protector," she would say, squeezing my pale and puny arm.

We would walk together until we hit the sand, and then she would go her way and I would go mine. I read books. I dozed. I took in the sun.

At eight am, on the sixth day of our trip, I staggered downstairs to the kitchen and began to arrange breakfast for myself. I had just thrown six kippers, sizzling, into the frying pan, when I heard the footsteps of a child running through the hall, accompanied by the more distant thud of adult feet, and various accompanying snarls and growls. I sighed to myself in dismay and turned my back to the kitchen doorway, so that if anybody should come in, I could pretend not to notice that they were there. As I flipped my kippers, I heard small feet come pattering into the kitchen and, suddenly, a searing pain shot through my right buttock. I turned to see a small blonde child and, behind her, a red-headed woman in her early thirties.

"Lily! Sorry, we were playing wolves. You know what they're like at that age. Energy to burn. Oh my God she's torn your trousers. I'm so sorry. Here I'll pay. I'll buy you a new pair. Lily! Stop clutching onto the man's leg."

"It's ok. I didn't think much of them anyway."

"Don't be silly. Here, I'll…"

She opened her wallet and a couple of coins fell out.

"Well, I'll go by the scash machine later."

"I'm fine, really. They're just old trousers that I only wear on holiday."

"You're staying here? I haven't seen you about."

"I've come here every year. For the last eleven years."

"Eleven years! Gosh. This is our first time. It's lovely, isn't it? Wonderful location. Right on the water. I'm Kate."

"Pleased to meet you," I said, without offering my own name.

She looked at her watch.

"Listen. What are you doing this morning?"

"Nothing. Eating breakfast. Hitting the beach."

She took in my sensible short-sleeved shirt, my grey cotton trousers, my expensive wristwatch (one small luxury in a lifetime of austerity).

"God. I hate to ask this. But you seem like a responsible kind of guy, so it's worth a shot. Would you mind helping me out? Just a little."

"What do you need?"

"I have to go to the supermarket to get some groceries for Lily and me. She hates it in there, always kicks up such a fuss. It's my fault. I took her to Sainsbury's once and then I forgot that I'd taken her along. I left her there by accident. Three hours on her own. When I went back, she'd climbed into the deep freeze and was cuddling a frozen chicken. Would you mind just looking after her for an hour or so?"

How had this happened? One minute a man's innocently cooking his kippers and the next he's lumbered with a child. I looked down at the angelic face staring up at me.

"Of course. No problem."

"Thanks. You're wonderful. I'll make it up to you, I promise. She's usually well-behaved with other people. It's just with me she plays up. Gets away with murder, sometimes. Well, I'd better run. I'll meet you back here at midday. Is that okay?"

She was gone before I could answer.

I fed the child half my kippers. I took her to the beach. Put a hat on her head to stop the sun from burning. Held her hand and took her paddling in the shallows. It was only at midday, when I walked Lily up the steps to the backpackers to meet her mother that I realized I'd forgotten all about escorting Felicity from her hotel to the beach. I could feel her fury already, piping hot, like the sand. For how long could I avoid her in a place this size? She would hunt me down, sniff me out, make an example of me. Fear made my stomach contract and my mouth grow dry. I sat close to Lily, waiting for Kate, attempting bravery.

Lily and I had been sitting outside the hostel for fifteen minutes when the child's mother came struggling, disheveled up the stairs, a bag of groceries under each arm. I ran down to meet her, took the bags from her, carried them inside. Child and mother trailed after me.

"Thanks so much for looking after her. You're a godsend."

"It's nothing really. It was a pleasure. She was no trouble at all. Very well behaved."

"Listen. Let me take you out to dinner. To be frank, I can't afford anywhere expensive, but I *can* afford to shout you a pizza. Do you have a favourite pizza place you want to go to?"

"I haven't tried the pizza out here."

"You haven't tried the pizza?"

"I haven't been to any of the restaurants."

"You've been coming out her for eleven years and you haven't tried any of the restaurants?"

I didn't know what to say. How to explain that I preferred not to live, but to avoid life? Hiding in its dark corners, shrinking from the light like a troglodyte, skulking at the periphery of my life. Running from the action. Being alive had always seemed to me a futile, pointless exercise. Escapism was my solution to the problem of existence; I escaped into numbers, calculations, formulae. Problems that could be managed, controlled. Questions for which there was always an answer. Never heard of a database that changed its mind, criticized you, stood you up.

She derailed my train of thought.

"That's ridiculous. Come on. Meet me down here at eight."

"I only brought the one pair of trousers. I travel light."

"We're not going anywhere flash. You'll be alright with the torn pants. Nobody's going to care. Come on, lighten up. You're on holiday! Jesus, man. Live a little."

The three of us sat together in one of the pizza restaurants, with their white plastic tables and chairs, their red and white chequered tablecloths, their burnt stubs of candles and carafes of cheap red wine, that were so ubiquitous in this neck of the woods. The waiter handed us the menus and I was just deciding between Neopolitana and Marguerita when I felt a familiar hand upon my shoulder. I looked up and saw that she wore no more than a gold bikini and a pink sarong. She was finally on her way home from the ocean.

"What happened to you this morning then? I was waiting for forty minutes."

"Nothing," I mumbled.

"Nothing? You leave me waiting for forty minutes and you call that nothing?"

"I forgot."

"You forgot?"

"Hi, I'm Kate," said my dining companion.

Lily just stared.

"Pleased to meet you," my sister said, extending an icy hand.

"Likewise."

"Well, since I see you have found *entertainment*, I'd best be moving on. Will I be seeing you tomorrow morning?"

"Of course," I said. "Usual time."

"Be prompt," she snapped, before sashaying off down the road.

"Who was that?" hissed Kate, following her departure.

"My sister. We come here together, but she stays in a hotel. She doesn't like the backpackers."

"Your sister? You come on holiday with your sister?"

I shrugged.

"It's tradition," I said, deciding to take a risk on the Neopolitana. "Can we order now?"

Walking to the beach the next morning Felicity said, "She'd never like a man like you. God, do you have any idea how incredibly *dull* you are? What makes you think that any woman would ever be interested in you? Why do you flatter yourself?"

"I think she likes me for my dullness."

"She's just using you, and you're too stupid to see it. What has she got you doing? Paying for dinner? Looking after the kid? Christ! You know what mother used to say – all the brains in the world and no common sense."

"I've got plenty of common sense. I'm a very logical man."
"There a world of difference between common sense and logic! You don't know how to exist in the world."
"I've done okay for myself. Not an exciting life, but then who needs…"
"So if you don't need excitement don't go chasing solo mothers!"
"I wasn't chasing."
"You were having dinner."
"She was thanking me."
"Thanking you? What for?"
"Looking after Lily."
"I knew it! You're such a dope. Well, dope, this is where I'm going to lie today, so take yourself somewhere else."
She spread out her towel and lay down upon it. I shrugged, gave her a small smile, then scurried back to the backpackers to cook breakfast for the three of us.

"Oh lovely," Kate smiled as I put an omelette in front of her and another, smaller plate in front of her daughter.
"Yum," said Lily appreciatively and stabbed at the food with her fork.
I sat down opposite them and watched them feeding, a mother and her cub in a nature programme nobody was filming.
"Listen," said Kate, halfway through the meal. "I know this might be cheeky of me, but do you have a driver's licence? I thought we could hire a car. Drive to Malaga. Check out the new Picasso museum. What do you say? This place can get a little claustrophobic after a while."
I smiled and nodded. I was an acquiescent man. I always seemed to be smiling or nodding. Or both.

I paid for it. I offered. She'd nearly run out of money. It was just a cheap little thing, a tin can on wheels.
"Right hand side of the road," she kept reminding me, as we drove the distance to Malaga, as if she feared I might forget myself and stray to the wrong side through sheer absent mindedness.

She played loud music on the car stereo and Lily beat her little fists on the back of my seat, in time. The two of them sang along, their windows wound down, the sun beating in upon us. As we drew near the city, Kate took a map from her handbag and began giving directions, navigating me neatly to a parking space two blocks over from the museum.

The paintings hung like trophies on the walls.
"A visionary," Kate declared, as we strolled through the rooms. "Pity he was such an asshole. All those women. Used. Doesn't stop me liking his paintings though. It's healthy to differentiate between an artist and his work, don't you think?"
"Or *her* work," I added.
"Yes, but just because you like somebody as a person, doesn't mean you necessarily like what that person produces. And just because you like what a person produces doesn't mean you have to like the person. Don't you think?"
I didn't really have an answer for that.

In a nearby café I bought three lemonades. Halfway through her drink, Kate stood up abruptly, said 'hang on a sec' and all but ran down the road, leaving me there with her daughter.
"Where's Mummy gone?"
"No idea."
"Can I have another lemonade?"
"Here," I said, to keep her quiet. "Have the rest of mine."
"But you might have germs."
"What kind of germs?"
"Boy germs."
"I'm not a boy."
"Are you a girl?"
"No. Not last time I checked."
"What are you then?"
"I'm a man," I said, only half believing the words.
"Have you got man germs?"
"No," I said. "Here. I'll pour some into your glass."
Kate was back within minutes, allaying my fears that she had left forever, abandoning both Lily and me.
"Here," she said. "I bought you something."

She handed me a cardboard tube.

"Come on! This is silly! You don't have any money, you can't buy me presents."

"Just a small token of our appreciation."

I pulled the plastic cap from the tube and peered inside. A roll of thin cardboard lay within.

"What is it? What is it?!"

Lily was out of her chair like a shot, standing next to me, pulling at the tube.

I reached inside and drew out the contents. It unfurled to reveal a blue Cubist cat holding a bedraggled, angular bird in its jaws.

"Wounded Bird and Cat," said Kate. "One of my personal favourites. I used to have a copy of it up in our flat. Till Darren ripped it in half one night, in one of his typical rages. I thought you might like it too."

"It's lovely," I said, unsure of whether or not I had chosen an appropriate adjective.

"You're everything he wasn't."

"Who wasn't?"

"Lily's father."

"Where is he now?"

"God knows. He doesn't pay any maintenance. I never want her to know him. He left when she was nine months old. Well, I kicked him out."

"Oh dear."

"Sometimes these fiery men seem exciting to you when you're younger. Then you get on a bit and you look for something different in a man. Some stability. Some brains. Some goddamned common sense."

"I see."

"Actually I tried to kick him out, but he wouldn't leave. One day we were fighting and he hit Lily as a way of hurting me, so I grabbed a suitcase and ran to my mother's. Started again from there."

"I would have done the same thing."

"Smacking me was one thing, but smacking Lily was another. Do you know what I mean?"

"Of course," I said. "I know exactly what you mean."

"Empathy is such an appealing trait in a man," she said, reaching over to give my hand a squeeze. "Remind me to give you my details tomorrow, before you go. It would be nice to meet up back in London."
"Yes it would," I squeaked.

We returned the car to the hire company and walked back along the beach in the direction of the backpackers. When Lily grew tired we sat down together on the sand and watched the last of the sunbathers leaving the beach. I felt her presence before I saw her.
"Oh hello there," she said, tightening her sarong. "What have you three been up to then?"
"Nothing," I said.
"What's this?"
She took the print from me, pulled it from its cardboard tube and unfurled it. The sun was setting behind her, giving her a shadow that seemed impossibly long.
"Oh," she said. "Picasso. Getting all cultured are we?"
Kate shifted uncomfortably. Felicity eyeballed her for a second, and then moved in for the kill.
"The thing is *sweetie*," she said, giving sarcastic emphasis to the word. "You wouldn't know how to treat him. You think he's so ordinary. But he's weird. He's fragile. He hasn't been the same since mother died. You know what happened, don't you? Went missing. For three weeks. To this day, nobody knows where he was all that time. We only know where he was when we found him. In the woods. Scrabbling in the dust, eating dirt. Howling at the moon. Only kept his job 'cause he had tenure. In any *normal* line of employment he'd have been out the door in two seconds flat. They cut his lectures and invented research assignments for him. It's only just last year he was actually allowed to teach again. He was *so* close to mother. Unhealthy, really. I've always tried to encourage him to have a life of his own, but I really don't think he's capable of it."
Kate said nothing.
"Well," concluded Felicity. "Don't say I didn't warn you."
And she continued on her way.

That night, Kate and Lily went to bed early and I sat out on the balcony and stared at the stars until three am when I fell asleep on the hard wood, waking with the dawn, and stumbling back to my room for more sleep. When I woke it was well past noon. I walked down the corridor to the room where Kate and Lily stayed. The door stood open. The room was empty. I walked to the ocean and stood on the sand, alone beneath an indifferent sky. The sun didn't care. It shone regardless, relentless. Inside my chest, something dripped and broke. Something slid down into my shoes.

I picked up Felicity in a taxi and we drove out to the airport. On the plane, we sat next to each other; she took the window seat though it had been allocated to me. When the air steward came round with his trolley, she ordered a double gin and tonic with a twist of lemon for herself and, when I didn't speak up to indicate my choice of poison, she spoke for me.
"He's fine," she said. "He doesn't want anything. He doesn't need anything."
The steward continued down the aisle.

## BLINDNESS

Harry had once had another name, something unpronounceable and Hungarian that he refused to share with us. He said that he wanted to speak only English, and seemed to think that his transition to the mother tongue must necessarily include a change of name. He said he still dreamt in Hungarian. He was missing two fingers; the severance of digits was an occupational hazard. Harry was a butcher. It was not a family tradition; there had been no real family from which a tradition could be inherited. Harry's father had flown the coop months before his birth and his mother was not on speaking terms with any of her family. According to my father, Harry had come to New Zealand to get away from his mother, who had bats in the belfry; he'd had spent a good deal of his life looking after this woman and had wanted to escape. We never discovered how Harry and his mother had supported themselves, but it was thought that, even as a young child, Harry had been forced to go out to work, performing some unspecified but undoubtedly unsavoury form of labour. Tired of his role as his mother's leaning post, Harry had arranged for a nurse to visit her twice a week, packed a suitcase and left. His sixteenth birthday was the day of his departure. The other side of the world was his destination.

The boat trip had taken six weeks. Harry was a lad with a cast-iron stomach and the constant motion did not bother him. He liked it; it was the opposite of the stasis in which he had been mired. It felt like progression. He didn't mix with the other passengers, but kept himself to himself, reading on deck, history books mostly, or war stories. He dined alone, wolfing down the slop they served up in huge, greedy mouthfuls. He did not have a cabin; physical privacy was a luxury for the rich. Harry, however, had mental privacy, a wall that he had erected years ago in order to keep his mother's demons, which had spilled from her psyche and flooded through all the rooms of the small house they had shared, from invading his mind. Upon arriving in Aotearoa, Harry, flat-broke but full of dreams of starting his own butchery, found gainful employ at the local freezing works, hacking up various corpses that were considered fit for human consumption.

Harry was all ears. He absorbed the language, took it in osmostically; the new words flooded in through his pores.

*Hello, how are you, goodbye. Gidday, how's it going, see ya later.*

Harry loved the way the words sounded, and would practice alone at night in his room, checking his reflection in the mirror to see how he looked when he spoke this new language; the language of the powerful, the language of prosperity.

"So many animals in this country," Harry remarked to a fellow worker, one day. "So many sheepses."

The co-worker smiled, and did not correct the grammatical error, but, feeling kindly towards this outsider, invited him home to his mother's house for a Sunday roast.

The fellow worker, who took a shine to this brave man who had travelled so far in a time when travel was neither cheap nor easy, was my father. A stranger in a strange land, Harry was graceful despite his bulk, and a remarkably conscientious worker, putting in the overtime, saving hard and spending little. Harry seemed strong and brave and admirable.

My father was not the only one who harboured affection for the new kid in town; his younger sister, Bertha, found herself admiring the large man's dedication, his good manners, the way he steadily held her gaze as he passed the gravy. They began taking long walks together, rambling along the beachfront, with Harry stumbling blindly through the English language, looking for the light switch, wrestling New Zealand idioms until he had pinned them to the floor of the ring. Bertha gently corrected his mistakes.

The age of sixteen was, for Harry, the age of maturity, the day when the locked door of adulthood swung open, and, when Bertha hit this landmark, Harry, somewhat predictably, proposed.

My father's own interest had been attracted, and held, by the young woman who delivered the mail to the freezing works each morning. It was a traditionally male role (*ha ha*, thought my father, *no pun intended*) and he respected this mailwoman for her guts, her balls, for having the courage to walk the streets each morning with her sack full of letters and parcels, braving vicious dogs and wolf whistles, before jumping behind the wheel of the mail truck and delivering the remaining items to out-of-town destinations, such as the freezing works. He always tried to time his cigarette breaks with her arrival; he loved to watch her climb down from her truck and stride purposefully towards the main office. She was the opposite of Bertha, frail Bertha, who had been a sickly child, and had remained thin, like a twig you could all too easily snap. Harry would protect Bertha, thought my father, provide a good home. Upon hearing of his sister's engagement, my father, not wanting to be left behind, made it his mission in life to convince the mailwoman to marry him, and after wooing her with many a drink in the local pub, finally achieved his goal.

The joint wedding had been Bertha's suggestion. They tied the double knot on a glorious spring day as the pohutukawa were beginning to bloom and the tuis sang in the trees and the world was the right way up.
"Pohutukawa," murmured Harry, on the way to the church. "Tui bird. Kakapo the parrot. Pull the other one, mate, it jangles."

Harry opened his butchery soon after the short honeymoon he'd enjoyed with his new wife in Gore. Bertha was soon pregnant with the embryo that was to become my cousin, Jake, and the mail woman was soon pregnant with me. The lives of Harry and my father, which had begun such a distance apart, on opposite sides of the earth, now ran parallel, two railway tracks, stretching out to the far horizon. No news was heard of Harry's mother, who may as well have ceased to exist upon Harry's departure from his native land. The two couples were still young enough to believe in an easy, uncomplicated life, in an existence that was simple and good. Experience had taught Harry that perseverance overcame problems, that no difficulty was insurmountable. But ahead there was a twist in the track; there were gaps in Harry's wall that he did not, or could not, mend.

I was seven when I learnt of Harry's impending blindness. Just as he had finally attained a firm grasp on the English language, his sight was slipping away from him. He complained of large black spots dancing before his eyes, obscuring his view of the world.

"Like great, dark angels," he said. "Like blackbirds. Like vultures."

He had, by this time, a fairly wide vocabulary.

He visited two GPs and a specialist. Nobody had a clue.

"No cataracts, no glaucoma, no macular degeneration," said the specialist. "Lord knows what's wrong with him."

"Silly little tyke," retorted Harry. "Robbing Peter to pay Paul."

Bertha would sit at our kitchen table and weep.

"Why is God punishing me like this? I've been a good woman, a faithful wife. Why did his sight have to leave him?"

"Maybe it's psychological," my mother replied one day.

I was in the next room with my ear pressed to wall. I didn't know what psychological meant, but it didn't sound good.

"Oh no," pleaded Bertha. "Don't say that, never say that."

My mother muttered something inaudible.

Harry gathered the darkness about him like a cloak. He stopped working, said that he couldn't see what he was chopping, where lay his fingers, and where the meat, and surely it would be dangerous to continue, given the circumstances. My mother found Bertha a job sorting mail; the frail became the breadwinner, the protector.

The people from the other place began arriving soon after Bertha went out to work. They came in twos and threes, marching through the living room of Harry's mind, whispering their cruel indictments, hissing their harsh judgements. They spoke not in English, but in Hungarian.

"How could you have left her behind?" they questioned accusingly. "Without even so much as a letter home, from time to time, to tell of your exploits."

"But I did send letters," Harry would protest, lying to these figments of his disturbed imagination. "Maybe they were just never delivered."

"It's no good," declared Bertha, who, after several weeks of sobbing, had become resigned, composed, bitterly practical. "He's losing his marbles. It's as simple, or as complicated, as that."

"Perhaps," suggested my mother, "he has traded his earthly vision for another kind of sight."

My father said that Harry should buck up his bloody ideas, snap out of it, pull himself together.

When Bertha could stand no more of Harry's inertia and madness, she and Jake moved into our spare room. She kindly arranged for a nurse to visit him twice a week, and would sometimes venture round with meals on plates. Beneath the Gladwrap with which she covered the food, she tucked little cardboard tags, with M, Tu, W, Th, Fri written on them to indicate when each should be eaten, as if to consume the meals out of order would throw the entire universe out of whack.

"Gladwrap. Watties. Dairy board," Harry would mutter in appreciation.

"See you soon," his wife would say, patting his shoulder. "Don't forget to wash."

"Bringing home the bacon," he would reply. "She'll be right, mate."

Harry was eventually institutionalised. We would visit him, from time to time. He thought he was back in Hungary, and would tell us of his recent visits to the Buda Castle, of the lengthy walks he had been taking along the Danube River, of crossing the Chain Bridge.

"No wall, no more," he would mumble from time to time. "Ka mate Ka mate, Ka ora Ka ora."

'Tis death, 'Tis death, 'Tis life, 'Tis life. My father would talk to him of the freezing works, and Bertha would speak of the honeymoon they had taken together in Gore and of his son, who grew a little taller, a little broader, with each passing day. No words, no phrase, no recollection, could jolt him back to reality. The people from elsewhere twittered constantly in Hungarian, a soundtrack Harry could not switch off. One of the doctors had given him a white cane, and when our visits were over, he would tap his way back down the corridor to his room, which he referred to as his 'cell', and we would shake our heads and murmur that it was such a shame to see him go to seed in this way. And we would wonder what he meant when he muttered about the wall.

## THE EEL

Early last summer my mother disappeared for good. I say 'disappeared', but what I really mean is that she left us, my brother Corey and me. There was a note, penned on the back of an old envelope and pinned to the fridge with a Donald Duck magnet; 'Kids – I need a change of scene and have gone elsewhere for a spell. Please don't take it personally. And don't try to follow me. Will send postcard soon. X Mum.'
What I remember thinking was, *Don't flatter yourself that we would bother to follow you. If you want to go, then go. Don't let trivialities like your own children hold you back.* Neither Corey nor I said anything out loud, we just stared silently at the note, until eventually I ripped the envelope from the door and threw it in the bin. Then I opened up the fridge and poured us both a long, cool drink of milk. I knew that she was never coming back. Two weeks later, Corey told me about the new swimming hole he had discovered.

We were watching *The Dukes of Hazzard* on TV. Stan had gone out for the evening – to his mate's for a booze-up, or to the pub, or down the betting shop. Stan wasn't our real father, he just happened to be our mother's live-in boyfriend the week that she decided to leave. Stan was a pig; he watched TV with a beer in one hand and the other down his pants, like Al Bundy. To me he didn't even seem human – he was more like something that had just crawled out of the primordial soup. 'Love' was tattooed across the knuckles of his left hand in dark blue ink; 'Hate' was tattooed across the knuckles of his right. The ink was dark blue, almost black. Squid ink. 'Mum' graced his left shoulder, the letters intertwined with what appeared to be some sort of rambling rose. The ink had bled on all three of his tattoos; it leaked to fill the wrinkles in the surrounding skin. We weren't happy about being lumped with him, and you could tell that he hated us. Stan was on the dole, he'd never worked a day in his life. My mother had provided him with food and shelter; he didn't have a house of his own. Now that she had gone, he lingered on with us because he had nowhere else to go.

Nobody knew where our biological father was; he'd left on Corey's seventh birthday, his gift had been his departure, his back receding down the driveway. He'd been a glazier – his van was parked up behind the garage, rusting. The van was white with *Parker's For Windows and Doors* written in green paint on the side. For a while, after he'd left, I'd put a mattress in the back of it and slept out there, trying to get away from something nameless. Then winter had drawn in with a vengeance, and I'd moved back into my old room, the one I shared with my brother, comforted by the familiar sound of him snuffling in his sleep. The walls of our room were completely covered in posters; Star Wars, Star Trek, Madonna. War posters - a coy blonde surrounded by interested gents with *Keep Mum She's Not So Dumb* written underneath. *Careless Talk Costs Lives.* Fighter planes ripping through the sky, trailing black smoke - *Back Them Up.* You couldn't see the wallpaper anymore, we'd hidden every square inch of it. This was a good thing; the paper beneath was ripped to shreds with the scrim poking through. Unsightly.

When Corey made his announcement he was lying on his stomach on the floor, with his chin resting in his hands. I was perched on the sofa, sipping one of Stan's beers that I'd nicked from the fridge.

"I've found a great new swimming hole," my brother declared. "Nobody else seems to know where it is. It's always deserted. It's way up the valley, further than we've ever been before."

The Dukes sped across a dusty orange landscape, giving chase or being chased – it was hard to tell which; the footage never showed both cars at once, just one then the other. Either car could have been out in front.

"Hmm?" I murmured absent-mindedly.

I was imagining that I was Daisy Duke, blonde hair fluffing in the breeze, long shapely legs that seemed to go on forever, flitting round town in small denim shorts, leaping neatly through car windows, not having to bother with doors.

"I found it on D-Day. I was up there on my bike."

'D-Day' stood for Departure Day – the day of our mother's disappearance. He *had* gone off for a long time on D-Day, I'd been worried about him.

"I'll show you," he continued. "After Hazzard's over."
"Yeah sure," I said. "Whatever."
A bee from one of our mother's hives flew in through an open window and landed on my arm. I swatted it dead with a nearby book.

The swimming hole wasn't as far up the river as he'd made out. From the way he spoke of it, you'd have thought it was miles upstream, but the truth was that we only had to bike for forty minutes to reach it. It was worth every push of the pedal, it was a little slice of paradise, wide and deep, cool and empty, surrounded by pines, enclosed. There were rapids at one end and, along the side, a series of staggered ledges for jumping off, higher and lower rocks. We leapt. It was deep where we landed, so deep that you couldn't even see the bottom, just your feet kicking about like frantic fish.
"Amazing," I yelled to Corey.
"Told ya," he said. "Thought you'd like it."
"Just think. If D-Day hadn't happened you never would have found it. So maybe it's a good thing that she left."
"Yeah," he said. "Right on."
But he didn't sound too convinced.

Late that night, we heard Stan come home and throw up in the kitchen sink. The stench of alcohol and vomit wafted down the hallway and under the doorway of the room in which we slept. Corey's voice came twisting up out of the darkness.
"Can't we get rid of him somehow?"
"I know," I replied. "It's not as if he contributes anything to the household."
      The day before, I'd sat the old slob down at the table and asked him if he could help out with the rent money.
"Rent?" he'd asked incredulously, and stared hard at me. "Rent's not my responsibility. Your mother always used to take care of that side of things. You're a big girl now. Go fend for yourself."
He'd risen up from the table, wandered across to the fridge, taken out a beer, downed it in two long swallows, burped twice, thrown the can in the sink and gone back to bed.

Our mother hadn't earned much, but it had been enough. She'd worked five hours a day, seven days a week, as a cleaner at the local fish factory. Free seafood was the only perk of the job. Our freezer was chock full of cod, smoked mussels, jellied eels. That's all there was left now – Stan's beer and a whole lot of seafood that my mother had never had to pay for.

"I just don't understand why she had to go."

Corey's voice again, slicing through the night. He'd been a good little trooper so far; this was the first time he'd complained aloud about our abandonment.

"There must be a reason," I said. "There's a reason for everything."

I wasn't at all sure that this was true, but it seemed a soothing, mature, thing to say. I had made up my mind to act like an adult until that mysterious day, located at some unspecified point in the future, when I would actually become one. The truth was that I was drifting, aimless. I had just finished high school and was at a loose end. I had no idea what I was going to do with the rest of my life. During the final week of school, everybody else had seemed so sure of themselves, so certain and unwavering in their plans; hairdressing college, medical school, a job in the local gas station. It didn't matter what it was – the point was that, for them, there was *something there*, whereas for me, the future was just blank space, a gap. I felt as if I was waiting for something to find me, for a golden index finger to tap me on the shoulder and point me in the right direction, for some long-forgotten voice to whisper in my ear. Nobody tapped; nobody whispered. The clock just ticked on, the same old life, as stale and stagnant as a mosquito breeding ground. The days seemed to stretch out endlessly, without beginning, without end; summer holidays forever. Maybe I would never become an adult, maybe my whole life would be nothing more than mimicry. Method acting.

It was then that Corey asked the real question.

"How are we going to make money?"

"I'll have to get a job," I replied.

What else could I say? I dreaded the prospect of employment. I'd been useless at school - I had problems concentrating. My mind had a tendency to roam. I was a tomboy; I would climb the most difficult tree and perch forever on the highest branch, I had built my own raft and gone sailing down notoriously treacherous rivers, I would set out into the woods hunting animals that probably didn't even exist – at least, not in this country. I ran wild. The teachers had tried to tell my mother that I suffered from Attention Deficit Disorder, but she hadn't bought it.

"She's just not interested," Mum'd told my form teacher when she'd bothered, once, to attend a parent-teacher evening. "It's not her cup of tea."

"What's not her cup of tea?"

"Education."

I'd scraped by. In tests and exams, if I didn't know the answers, I would just make something up. I wrote a lot, filled up the books allocated and then some, but all of it was garbage. Most teachers didn't have the heart to fail me, they would look at those words, all those scribbled lines and give me a low pass. They'd probably never even bothered to read what I wrote. Now it was time for me to reap the lack of knowledge I had sown; time to head out into the workforce, unskilled and ignorant.

"What about the hives?" Corey said. "Those bees are ours now. We could steal their honey and sell it."

"Hmm," I said. "Maybe. Let me sleep on it. But please don't worry, I'll think of something. Good night."

"Night," he replied. "Sweet dreams."

His voice sounded very small, as if it was coming from a great distance away.

I took a job in a local sandwich shop. It was easy work, just slapping fillings in bread for three hours each weekday morning. The only catch was that I had to start at four a.m. so that all pre-filled sandwiches were made by seven, when people would call by on their way to work. There was one advantage to my early morning shift - my working day was soon over and done with and the remaining hours belonged to me. Corey and I filled the time. We lay in the long grass in the field behind our house, listening to the cicadas sing. We held onto electric fences and felt the current flow through our bodies as it found its way to earth. We lifted the lid of the next door neighbour's well and peered inside. We swam.

Something lurked in the swimming hole. Corey felt it first. Just as the sun was starting to go down it brushed past his leg, turned, returned, and bit him hard on the ankle. He yelped and started swimming furiously towards the riverbank.

"It *bit* me," he yelped, as he hobbled up onto the rocks. "Something *bit* me."

"What did? What bit you?"

"*Something*. Something in there."

He pointed at the black murky soup of the water.

"You big wuss," I said. "It was probably just an eel. They come out to feed at dusk."

But Corey was young, prone to hysterics.

"*Get out*," he screeched. "Get out or it'll get you."

"For *God's sake*. Calm down."

I left the water, just to shut him up. I hated it when he lost his head. He sat down on a flat, grey rock and clutched his ankle, displaying the evidence. There were two small pinpoints of blood, there, on the inside, just above the anklebone, tiny, as if somebody had pricked him, twice, with the sharpest of needles. I crouched down next to him and put my arm around his shoulders.

"Eel fangs," I said. "Definitely. Come on now, stop being silly."

He gave a shuddering sort of sob and then said, uncertainly, "Yeah, I guess you're right."

He wiped away the blood with a towel, dried himself off and then stood for a moment, looking at the water, as if he expected something to come rearing up out of it. But the surface was calm, unbroken by ripples.

"Yeah," he said, as if repeating after me. "Eel fangs."

On the bike ride home, he was dangerously quiet.

At night, we plotted how best to rid ourselves of Stan. *Let's butcher him and bury him in the backyard*, we whispered. *Or drown him in the river, hold his head under until he stops breathing. Else put him in concrete boots, something heavy to sink him, take him down. Let him sleep with the fishes.*

We'd already tried the direct approach. I'd cornered Stan in the kitchen and told him that he had to leave.
"You're a drain on us," I said. "You're not paying any rent, *or* any of the bills and you're eating us out of house and home."
Stan was a garbage can, he chomped his way through anything edible he could find; he'd even eaten most of the jellied eels. His response to my criticism was so quick that it must have been pre-prepared.
"If you kick me out, I'll go to the cops and tell them your mother's gone. You know what'll happen then."
Threats hung like impending storms in his voice, but there was fear there also. He knew that he was walking a fine line; after all, I might want to get rid of him more than I wanted to keep Corey out of foster care. I was six years older than my brother – too old for them to take. But Corey was fair game. They could snatch him away. He would be shunted round foster homes, pushed on from place to place. No rest. No home. Always moving on. Stan'd clung to our mother like a leech, and now he was attempting to do the same to us. He was the kind of man who would slowly suck you dry and then move on to his next host; a parasite. He expected us, an eighteen-year-old and a twelve-year-old, to keep him. He didn't care how. He knew nothing of my sandwich job, he lay in bed most of the day.
"How do you intend to pay the rent, anyway?" he asked.
"Prostitution?"
The line grew a little finer.

It soon became obvious that the money from the sandwich shop would not be enough to live on. Corey's advice proved priceless - we started our business; the harvesting and selling of the honey. We were nothing if not entrepreneurial. The hives sat just behind our dilapidated garden shed; the bees zoomed to and fro, as if strung on invisible wires. Our mother had taken up and dropped many hobbies. 'Flighty' my real father had called her, shortly before he'd flown the coop himself. You name it, she'd tried it – pottery, stamp-collecting, thai chi, power yoga, glass-blowing and finally, the bees. The neighbours hadn't been keen on the bees, they'd said you weren't meant to keep them in built-up suburban areas. You needed a bigger section for that sort of thing, they said, more land. My mother hadn't listened; she wasn't big on listening to what other people said. She'd bought the hives and the smoker, the leather gloves, the hood and veil. She was good at it, beekeeping. I didn't recall many stings. She'd been good at everything, initially - it was sustaining interest that had been the problem for her. For weeks we'd had fresh golden honey, dripping from the comb. We ate it in the morning; dribbled it on Weetabix and fresh fruit and toast. She'd retrieved it for us herself, in a rare act of something that was almost like love. And now she was gone, she'd abdicated.

Neither of us had bothered to try and track our mother down - we had far too much pride. Besides which, we had no idea where she'd gone, she could have been anywhere. She'd abandoned us, that was all we knew; she had made good her escape. Corey and I spun fictions, speculating as to her whereabouts. She could've headed for the middle of nowhere, to some other country, gone into a land for which the maps had yet to be written. Or maybe she had escaped to some tropical paradise and lay there now, sunning herself, living off coconuts and pawpaws. Catching fish with her bare hands. Perhaps the note had been fraudulent - she'd been kidnapped, or rather, mother-napped. They'd held a gun to her head and told her what to write, and then she'd been brutally raped and buried alive somewhere. She'd claw her way out through the dirt one day, resurface with worms hanging off her and crawl back home, rise up from the dead, full of secrets that only those who had returned from under the mud could know. Or else she'd been abducted by aliens; they'd descended ever so stealthily in their mother ship, bug eyes bulging from their bulbous heads, elasticated limbs that could stretch for miles, speaking in their own weird code, a series of clicks and clacks, squeaks and curious scratching sounds. Some sort of sonar. They'd taken her as she lay sleeping; beamed her up.

Wherever she was, she never wrote. Corey checked the mail every day, but the promised postcard never arrived. He might have been waiting to hear from her, but I certainly wasn't. She was like a lost limb; gone, forgotten, severed. If she'd chosen to return I would have pretended not to know who she was. I had removed her from me, cut her out. She was dead to me.

But her bees weren't. She'd left all her gear behind – we found it in the back of the wardrobe in her old room. I withdrew a few books from the public library and we swatted up. It seemed easy enough to retrieve the honey – smoke the bees, remove the boxes, check that the honey has been capped, and if so, smoke the bees in the capped boxes again and remove the frames.

"Simple," said Corey. "You can do it, no sweat."

It was vaguely dangerous work. I dressed up in those garments that my mother had left behind, picked up the smoker. There were six hives in total; I started with just one, left the rest for later raiding. I was stung three times but it didn't really hurt. Victorious, I carried the frames into the house. We worked in the laundry; it didn't matter if we made a mess. We didn't have a spinner that we could use to extract the honey, so we just hacked off chunks of the comb, making as many neat squares as we could. The remaining fragments we crushed, and then strained through muslin. The comb went into old Chinese takeaway containers, the liquid honey was poured into glass jars.

Corey was still on vacation. Every lunchtime, Monday to Friday, we'd load the honey into backpacks and head for the business district, where we would hawk the golden produce to whomever was willing to buy it; two young hustlers on the make. At the weekend we set up a desk outside our house, and arranged a neat little display. Business was slower on these days, but we still managed to make a tidy little profit. And all of it tax free, under the table.

"God bless the bees," said Corey, after we raided the second hive.

But what would we do when the honey ran out?

"We need to take it all by the end of the summer," said Corey. "We'll just stock it up. Pray that it's enough to see us through the year."

We got by. I bought cheap fruit and vegetables from the local market, purchased extra-large bags of pasta, rice, spuds – staples. Something to see us through. In a way, we were strangely free, although the truth is that, in our short lives, we had known little restriction. Our mother's dubious attempts at parenting had involved lame, half-hearted attempts at imposing curfews (which were always ignored, with no resulting punishment), the setting up of boundaries that crumpled with the softest prod, threats that were never enforced. We had grown up in a world that was largely borderless, without limits, so the subsequent departure of our mother had not been as much of a shock as it might have been to those who had known firm parental guidance, had always understood exactly what was what and who was boss.

Certainly, we'd learnt how to be self-entertaining units. We'd taught ourselves all kinds of games; chess, backgammon, poker. There had been other activities, too. One Easter, we'd decorated eggshells and put them on display on the mantelpiece. The eggs had been raw; we'd poked holes in them with a needle and blown out the yolks and the whites. We'd painted up the shells and glued on brightly coloured beads and small shards of shattered mirrors. Later, we'd made an omelette with the eggs' insides.

At school, I'd seen girls walking around with egg babies. It was a home economics lesson; teaching them how to care. They made miniature baskets to carry their eggs in, sewed them little eggy outfits, gave them names. Every now and then, one of the clumsier girls would sit on her egg by accident and stand up with an ugly smear of yellow and white across the back of her skirt, or someone would leave their charge beside an open window, an accident waiting to happen, or somebody else's brother would smash her egg out malice. In one more spectacular death, a girl accidentally dropped her 'baby' from a bridge that crossed over the railroad tracks and the thing had been squished by a train. Anybody who killed their egg automatically got an 'F' for that particular module. This was a dreaded fate, the implication being that not only were you unfit to mother an egg, but that you were also unfit to mother a child. I never saw boys with eggs. Boys didn't do home economics – they were allowed to, of course, just as the girls were permitted to do metalwork, but none of them chose it, as to do so would have been to court mockery. A few rogue girls did metalwork; I was one of them. I made a flour scoop, a funnel, a fish slice.

Most eggs remained unbroken. Most girls passed. But their eggs were hard-boiled, solid; ours had been just empty shells. It had been our mother's boyfriend who had destroyed them. Not Stan, but a previous one, a hairy guy with bad breath and permanently reddened eyes from excessive pot smoking. He'd fallen asleep standing up, right next to the mantelpiece, keeled over, his elbow crushing what we had made. I watched it happen; slow-motion. Corey saw it too and started wailing. Mum had come in to see what all the fuss was about and my brother'd just pointed at the broken shells.

"Oh, stop your blubbing," Mum had said. "They were starting to smell anyway."

That was a lie; we'd been thorough when we'd blown out their insides. Corey had cried inconsolably, and there had been nothing I could do or say to make him stop, I just had to lie in bed and listen to him sob himself to sleep, knowing that it wasn't the first time and that it wouldn't be the last.

The thing in the water got me. We'd had a good day, sold a lot of honey and I was floating on my back, quietly gloating over our good fortune. It bit me, just as it had bitten my brother, on the inner ankle. No wonder Corey had cried out. It felt like somebody had punctured my skin with a hole punch. Something slimy flicked its tail and swam away.

"The bugger's at it again," I shouted. Get out of the water, Corey."

We scrambled up the bank, examined the damage. My wound was similar to his; the two neat fang marks, a vampire's deadly kiss. The mark of the beast. But they seemed bigger, these holes, too big for an eel, despite what I had said earlier. Corey looked at what had been done and shivered.

"It's getting territorial," he whispered. "C'mon, let's go home."

Now I was the one who was starting to get spooked.

"What is it?"

"Dunno," he said. "Don't ask. Something ancient."

There were further efforts made to actively discourage Stan from sponging off us, to convince him that he would be better off elsewhere. I changed the locks; he called in a locksmith and had new keys cut. I poured his beer down the sink; he clobbered me about the head and told me that if I ever did that again he would thrash me to within an inch of my life. I padlocked the fridge to try and starve him out; he hacksawed through the chain. There *was* no ridding ourselves of him; he was here to stay.

We kept away from the river at dusk. If we only swam in broad daylight, we reasoned, whatever was in the water wouldn't get us. We figured that it hid during the day, was allergic to the light. And we were right. As long as the sun was high in the sky, nothing ever happened. The sun kept us safe.

One Saturday, the monster awoke. It was nearly noon and Corey and I were sitting at our desk at the end of our driveway, trying to badger passersby into purchasing our honey, discussing whether or not we would go up the river that day. He came staggering towards us, muttering something inaudible, wearing only his underpants, fat gut bulging out over the top. I hadn't heard him come home at all the night before – it must have been later than late, the early hours of the morning. He was still drunk. You could smell it on him, wafting out in waves; he reeked like an old pub that hadn't been cleaned in over a century.
"Hello there," he said. "Hello there, Corey."
He leered at my younger brother, towered over him, dwarfing him with his bulk.
"What have we here then? Looks good."
He ripped the lid off one of the containers, lifted out a piece of comb honey and took a large, greedy bite. It dribbled down his chin like a glistening liquid beard.
"Mmm," he said. "Delicious. Gimme more."
He grabbed another two containers and made to tear off their lids. Corey lunged at him and bit him hard on the upper arm, just below the 'Mum' tattoo. My brother had very sharp teeth; when he pulled back you could see that he'd drawn blood. Stan howled and reeled and swiped at the desk like a clumsy, intoxicated bear. The desk tipped and overturned, jars smashed, honey oozed every which way. Corey left his senses.
"I want him to leave!" he screamed. "Why won't he leave?"

"What's wrong with you?" grunted Stan. "Got a bee in your bonnet?"
"We don't want you here," shouted Corey. "We want you to go!"
"Keep the little shit under control," Stan said to me. "Or I'm narking to the cops."
"Be quiet, Corey," I said, and attempted to pull him toward me. But Corey could not or would not be calm.
"Get him out!" he yelled. "This is *our* house. That fat oaf doesn't belong here."
I don't know whether it was the 'fat' or the 'oaf' that hit home, but something struck a discordant chord. Stan waddled back inside. Through the window, I saw him pick up the phone and dial.

The social worker came that Monday, with her clipboard and her blank file and her blue and red pens. She wore a name tag that read simply 'Betsy'. I stayed home from work, in order to stop them from taking Corey but, in the end, there was nothing I could do.
"There's no parental figure here," said Betsy. "We'll have to take him into care."
"What about me?" I asked, with two fingers clinging to the red T-shirt that Corey wore.
She looked at me and scoffed.
She took him then and there; there were no forms, there was no debate.
"Don't do what Mum did," I whispered to Corey, as he was led away. "Don't disappear. Let me know where you are – telephone or write. Stay in touch."
But Corey didn't say anything; he wouldn't even look me in the eye.
Stan was happy. He kicked back on the sofa, switched on the telly with the remote.
"Ah, the power of age," he said, as he lit a cigarette.

I stayed away from the swimming hole for good after that.

# PETS

I grew up in the middle of nowhere. A farm in New Zealand's King Country - the back of beyond. At the end of our property was a well that had been boarded over for as long as anyone could remember. To get to the well you had to high jump over three electric fences, taking care not to get zapped, then you had to cross a small river and not get your feet wet, then you had to pick your way through a patch of nettles, attempting not to get stung. Due care was always taken, but it was impossible to arrive at the well without having suffered a zap, or wet feet, or a sting. I made the journey daily. I liked the well; its depth, which was unknown (possibly bottomless), the crumbling bricks from which it was made, the planks that covered it. One of the planks was rotten; I would pull it off and stare down into the darkness. At times I imagined that there was something staring back.

Kathy Hutchinson lived on the farm adjourning ours. She was two years younger than I was. My sister Rachel and me thought she was spoilt and mean, a bully. If she didn't get her way, she would throw a tantrum and her mother would give in and let her have whatever it was that she wanted. Our cat, Mimi, had come from the Hutchinson household; he was vicious, wild - if you tried to pick him up he'd claw your eye out. We forgave him his temperament; we knew he'd suffered an abusive kittenhood at the hands of the Hutchinson girls, Kathy and her sister Leah. They'd pulled his tail and thrown him into buckets of cold water and shaved his fur and dressed him up in doll's clothing and, as a result, he'd become ferocious. It was his way of sticking up for himself, of warning people not to mess with him. Sometimes he would hunt our sheep, creep up behind one, jump onto its back, hang on with all four claws as if he truly believed he could kill and eat it. The lion within. The chosen sheep would sprint across the paddock with our cat clinging onto its wool; we laughed and took photos. We liked the cat - he was a character. Better that, we thought, than some docile moggy that provided no entertainment.

How old was I that day when, tentatively making my way through the stinging nettles, I saw Kathy standing by the well? Ten or eleven, twelve maybe. In her arms she had a black sack with something inside it, squirming. Dark clouds massed overhead like a flock of vultures. There was no love lost between Kathy and I. We'd had some wicked gravel fights; me and Rachel versus Kathy and Leah, standing in the Hutchinson's driveway, pelting each other with fistfuls of tiny stones. There had been other kids as well, joining in the festivities, swapping sides faster than Mussolini, until in the end it became an exercise in not being on the losing team, a simple matter of running across to stand with whichever group had the most people. I remembered one time when Kathy had been left on her own; whenever she tried to cross to the other side everybody else would leave her and go and stand opposite. She stood there throwing her feeble little handful of gravel while being pelted by our far larger hail of small stones. Bully as victim. I'd thought at the time that, despite my dislike of her, it was still mean, and that I should've had the guts to take her side when nobody else would, but I wasn't willing to stick my neck out for her, to take some of the stones. I didn't want to become a target myself.

The sack was meowing, though not the sack, of course, but what was inside it.

"Kathy?" I said, walking up to her slowly, as you would approach a wild animal or somebody who'd escaped from a mental hospital, or a cornered criminal who carried a loaded gun. "Kathy, what've you got in that sack?"

The question was rhetorical, I wasn't expecting an answer. I knew exactly who was in there, I recognised those meows.

"Kathy, put the cat down."

It was the tone of voice I'd heard cops on the TV use, *Put the cat on the ground, step away from the cat.* Kathy eyed me, she looked wild, slightly unhinged, you could tell she was remembering the gravel fight. Maybe she'd been here before, she seemed to already know about the rotting plank, because she pulled it away and held the cat above the gap. She gave me a smile that held a note of victory. Then she dropped the sack into the well. The sky broke and the rain began.

"Murderer!" I shouted.

I ran across to the well, shoved her out of the way. Mimi was thrashing about, keeping afloat, but only just.

"Bitch!" I yelled.

It was the first time I'd used the word; it wasn't something that was ever said in our house. I would've been smacked on the bum and sent to my room if one of my parents heard me say that word. It held no power here. Kathy just stared at me, her eyes hard, dead. There was a stick on the ground, I picked it up, fished inside the well, hooked it through the bag, retrieved the cat. I untied the knot at the top of the sack and beheld our family pet. He spluttered, coughed, stared up at me with wild frightened eyes then bit me hard on the arm and raced off across the paddock. Rage roared at the edge of my mind. "Get out of here Kathy," I hollered. "Nobody wants you here, you *cat murderer*. You *cat thief*. He's not *your* cat anymore, Kathy. You don't get to decide if he lives or dies!"

But still she didn't respond, just kept on staring at me, so I left her there and began heading back across the fields, through the rain, towards our house and it struck me, as I walked away, that throughout the entire weird episode, Kathy hadn't spoken a word.

A month or two later my parents decided that we would be leaving the farm. It was too much work, they said. Things were starting to get on top of them. They would move to Nelson, a sunny tourist town at the top of the South Island and start a B&B. They could make the same income, my father said, with a lot less effort. The farm was sold, the house was packed up. My sister and I were charged with putting kitchen goods into boxes. On one of the shelves we found a can of condensed milk dated 1974, which made it fifteen years old. When we opened it up we found that the milk had set in layers, a solidified yellow crust at the bottom, then lighter slop above that, with a fine watery liquid floating on the top. We examined it like archeologists, digging down through the sedimentary layers, prodding in the muck. Maybe we would find some kind of fossil in there, hiding at the bottom of the can.

The cat was fed tranquilisers and shoved into a box with eye holes cut into it. I put my face down to the box and saw his frightened green eyes with the dilated pupils peering out at the world. I tried to reassure him by putting one finger through an eye hole to stroke his head, but he just chomped down hard on my finger, made it bleed. It was my fault; I should've known better. If I was stuck in a box and somebody poked their finger inside I'd probably bite it too. The removal truck arrived to take our larger belongings; we piled into our Holden and began the journey South.

The ferry crossing was rough. Up on deck, people clutched at the railing, being violently ill into the ocean all the way to Picton, the small fishing town where the boat comes in. We drove our car down the ramp, parked up in the city centre, adjourned to a nearby pub for a meal. It was raining; a steady grey drizzle from the sky. Between mains and dessert, Rachel started shifting uncomfortably in her seat, sighing heavily through her nose.
"Rachel, what is it?" asked Mum.
"I feel sorry for the cat," she said. "He's been cooped up for ages. Can I take him for a walk?"
She took a piece of string from her pocket and said, "I can use this as a lead."
"Oh alright then. But be quick, just ten minutes. We'll save your dessert for you."
"Thanks Mum!"
And off she went, to provide some temporary relief for the trapped cat. She tapped on the pub window as she passed by, smiled and pointed down at our pet who strained to get away from her, his collar choking at his throat. Bemused looks from the locals. Five minutes later her voice came drifting through the rain.
"Dad, Daaad, help!"
She was down by the waterfront, clutching onto the end of the string. The cat had sprinted up a tree; he perched on the highest branch, uttering tortured sounds, his fur soaked flat against his skin. My father climbed up, brought him back to earth. We toweled him dry, but irreversible damage had been done. He was never the same way again.

The cat contracted pneumonia and was taken to the vet. It was touch and go. *Fifty-fifty,* said the vet. *Pray for him.* I did pray; I knelt at the end of my bed every night, muttering to a God that I didn't even know if I believed in and Mimi pulled through and then I decided that I did believe in God after all, for that was the pact I'd made - let the cat live and I promise to serve you in any way you like, even though I knew that it was wrong to make demands on God like that, that He moved in mysterious ways, did whatever He wanted, that you didn't say *I want this and I want that*, but that you asked nicely, *Please Sir, I know you're very busy right now, but if you could spare me a moment, I was wondering if maybe it would be possible to....* Whether He heard me or not, we'll never know, but Mimi pulled through. The cat was a trooper. He lived on for another seven years with one lung, wheezing as he breathed, his little furry body heaving up and down as he inhaled and exhaled.

Death came for him slowly. There were warning signs. I returned home from school to find him coughing up blood on the living room floor and told my mother that we should take him back to the vet, that he needed treating.

"Oh, don't be silly," she said. "He'll be alright."

But I knew that he wouldn't, I could see the grim reaper hovering just behind him, scythe raised, waiting to swoop.

My bedroom was next door to the laundry. One morning as I was waking, I heard my father being violently ill in the laundry sink and I knew that Mimi had died. He was laid out in a banana box in the garage and we all filed in to pay our last respects.

"He went peacefully," my father said, but when I saw the cat lying there, I found this hard to believe.

His face was set in a snarl and his paws were outstretched, as if fending something off.

"Bye Mimi," I said. "You've been a good cat. May you discover in the next world the peace that you couldn't find in this one."

We buried him down by the river, the site marked with a small white cross. The next week we read in the paper that Kathy Hutchinson had died in a diving accident near the Great Barrier Reef. She'd swum away from her buddy, run out of oxygen, suffocated there, in the deep blue sea.

"Terrible," said my father, as he read the article aloud. "Kathy Hutchinson, remember her? She was a nice little girl."

I held my tongue. What would I have to gain by correcting him?

"Yea," I said. "She was great. She gave us Mimi."

I didn't mention the time that she'd tried to drown the cat, or the gravel fights, or how rare it was to find somebody who would take the side of someone who was losing; though these are the things that remain with me, as memories stick in the mind like fossils in rock.

# PIANO LESSONS/WAR STORIES

Everything about my grandmother's piano was perfect. It was perfectly polished, perfectly upright, perfectly in tune. It was she who first taught me how to play – a kind woman who smelt of roses and talcum powder. She dressed in soft pastel colours, pinks and blues. She was sweet. She baked a mean pavlova. "Oh, I don't think this one's much good," she would say as she walked to the table with yet another perfect dessert – crisp crust, soft meringue, whipped cream, decorated neatly with kiwifruit and strawberries.

She would shrug her shoulders shyly when, licking their silver spoons, scraping clean their porcelain plates, everybody proclaimed how good it was.

"Must be the recipe," she would say. "My mother handed it down to me."

My grandfather was different. He had fought in the war and it had changed him, hardened him. He seemed severed from his emotions, slightly robotic, as if he was impersonating a person. He never spoke of what had happened when he was away, of the horrors he had seen, the deaths he had witnessed. Like all men of his generation, he kept a lid on it. He departed for the war one man, and came back quite another - left a substantial part of himself somewhere in the South Pacific. His sense of humour, however, had remained intact, and was drier than the Sahara Desert. He was hilarious, delivering his deadpan lines with a straight face, brown eyes twinkling.

He was our self-appointed censor.

"Time for the little ones to go to bed," he would say if, when watching television, anything so much as a kiss came on the screen, and my sister and I would traipse, giggling, up the stairs.

"Lights out!" my grandmother would call and, obediently, I would reach for the main switch.

Then we would read for another few hours, under the covers, with a torch; *The Lion, the Witch and the Wardrobe, Shadow the Sheepdog, Can I Get There By Candlelight? White Fang.*

It was my grandmother who gave me my first piano lessons. She would take me by the hand and lead me downstairs to where the instrument sat, in a clean, ordered room, with big wide windows that let in the light. Ebony sat against ivory like black marks upon a blank page. I was fascinated by all pianos; it sometimes seemed that all the songs in the world, all the songs that had ever been, or ever could be, were stored up inside them, just waiting for somebody to let them out.

I was tiny when the lessons started, barely three years old. I was always small for my age, always at the end of the line when the teacher stood the pupils in a row, ordered by height. Always first or last, depending upon from where you started counting. Imagine me then, my third birthday just gone, tapping away at my grandmother's Steinway. I did not sit upon the stool; I stood. My chin was level with the keyboard. When fully outstretched, my right hand spanned three keys. Nursery rhymes were my early lessons - *Three Blind Mice, Mary Had a Little Lamb, Itsy Bitsy Spider.* All the songs seemed to involve animals. Sometimes we sang along, and my grandfather would bash on the wall with a broom handle and shout *what's that caterwauling?* But we knew that he didn't mean anything by it.

The piano in our own entrance hall was not in the same league as my grandmother's – it was so old, so out of tune, that its atonality could not be rectified. Its wood was cracked, faded, and the instrument itself sloped dangerously to the right, as if it had been in an earthquake, had its base, its foundations, shaken out of joint. My mother had summoned the local piano tuner and, after tinkering for twenty minutes, he'd left shaking his head in dismay, having fixed nothing. The piano was beyond hope.

It came to serve a decorative purpose; my mother thought that it looked good, broke up the blank walls of the hall. Nobody was supposed to play it, but I just couldn't seem to leave it alone. I would learn tunes at my grandmother's house, then go back home and practice them. Played on that particular piano, they sounded creepy, haunting, wrong. Alone at that old atonal instrument, I always felt strangely disassociated from myself, as if my soul had detached itself from my body and floated up high, near a corner of the ceiling, looking down, watching. Sometimes it seemed as if the piano was playing by itself. Perhaps it was possessed.

My sister seemed to think so. She used to claim that she'd heard it, when she'd been locked out, after school one day. "Swear to God," she said. "I was standing just outside the front door and I heard it playing Beethoven's *Hammerklavier* – a wonderful sonata."

Who was Beethoven?

"Some old guy. Went deaf."

I knew she was lying, making it up. Where would she have heard this sonata, how could she have recognised it? Nobody in our family played classical music; my father listened to the Beatles, Bob Dylan, Elton John. No doubt she'd heard about Beethoven and his 'Hammerklavier' somewhere else, at school, or in the street, or on the radio, and was trying to sound knowledgeable, attempting to creep me out with talk of the possessed piano. I refused to be afraid. I had nothing to fear from the spirit world. If there *were* ghosts inside that instrument, I would win them over, make friends. New pets.

Our ancient instrument had one advantage over my grandmother's – you could pull it apart. There was a panel below the keyboard that you could remove with the aid of a screwdriver; this would expose the strings, which you could then pluck at, like playing a harp. That was fun. When he wanted me out of his hair, my father would take away that panel, and I would get in there with a comb and run it back and forth along the strings, create a right ruckus. And that's all there was, inside that piano – just strings and nothingness. There were no ghosts. Any idiot could see that.

There were ghosts in my grandfather though; he was haunted by all those soldiers who hadn't made it, by those who had fallen. Sometimes, when my sister and I stayed overnight with our grandparents, he would wake up yelling, and we would hear my grandmother calming him down, going to the kitchen to prepare him a glass of hot milk, something to soothe his nerves. His shouts were sharp; they split the night like bullets. Nothing could stop his nightmares - not his whisky nightcap, not his wife rubbing his back, not the milk.

Years later, it came out, there had been one soldier, his best friend, who had told him to continue even though he, the friend, couldn't go on, couldn't be bothered fighting, cracked, broke, shot himself in the head right in front of my grandfather. It was fear that did him in; fear and fatigue. He had been convinced that they would be caught by the Japanese, for that's who they were fighting, out there in the ocean, near Fiji. They were notoriously vicious, the Japs. To be captured by such an enemy would have been a fate worse than death. It didn't bear thinking about, what they would do to you. A third of their POWs died in their camps; they were war criminals. You'd stand a better chance if you were captured by the Germans. As long as you weren't a Jew, that is.

It was my grandmother who got that out of her husband, eventually, some fifty years after the war had ended, pulled it out of him, like an old thorn. Held it up to the light for all the family to examine, as if she was saying, 'look, this is the reason and now we have removed the reason and he will be fixed.' But of course, it didn't work that way – the wound remained, thorn or no thorn. The damage done. Besides, there were bound to be numerous other 'reasons', other thorns - shrapnel embedded too deeply to ever be removed.

When I was older, thirteen, fourteen, I took official piano lessons from a dusty old woman in a dusty old house. The light in that room was so bad that I could barely see the keys, could hardly see my hands moving across them. The teacher had a ruler that she would use to bash my knuckles with if I played a bum note; would bring it smashing down, *crack*, a sound like wood being split with an axe. I would return home with horrid red marks on the backs of my hands and complain to my mother about the harsh treatment I was receiving. She would shrug and say, *well, how else are you going to learn?* She refused to take my side. She was paying good money for the lessons; she wanted me to emerge a prodigy, a pubescent maestro, she didn't care how much suffering and bashing of the knuckles would be involved, paid no mind to the price I paid. She wanted to get her money's worth. She didn't seem to notice, when I practised at home, that my playing was clunky, heavy-handed, full of clumsy errors and slips of the fingers. I lacked lightness of touch. I did not play, I hammered. The keys were a series of anvils. And everything out of tune - we could only just afford the lessons; a new instrument was out of the question. My mother seemed to cling to some strange dream, a curious vision of me travelling the globe, seated comfortably at a Baby Grand, delighting enraptured audiences with a charming rendition of *Appassionata* or *Pathétique* or the *Moonlight Sonata. Hammerklavier*.

I feared the piano teacher – who wouldn't? Often I would skip lessons and wander round the neighbourhood for an hour instead, stealing mail out of other people's letter boxes, plucking blooms from the botanic gardens, peering through the windows of the Museum of Natural History. Or I would sit down by the railway tracks and watch the trains whistling by, wishing that I was going somewhere, anywhere, I didn't care where. The journey, not the destination, was the point.

I didn't want to learn what the mad old biddy taught me anyway, didn't want to progress steadily up through the grades, sitting the yearly exam, taking part in the annual concert. I preferred to go to my friend's house, where I would tackle pieces that were far too advanced for my abilities. I did not want to aim for, and reach, the highest branch of the tree; I'd rather shoot for the stars and risk falling. At home, I would play the first few bars of *Fur Elise* over and over, as if my hands were trapped in a loop of time. It must have driven my parents mad, but they never said anything. Every now and again, I would make up a little tune of my own – nothing fancy.

Shortly after his seventieth birthday, when I was in my final year of high school, my grandfather had his first heart attack. It struck him down while he was at bowls; death reaching a long black hand inside his chest and giving his ticker a good, solid squeeze. He fell to the ground, as if he had been struck by lightning, twitched, and was still. They called an ambulance. It was not too late. He was rushed to hospital for an emergency angioplasty – on the way there they gave him CPR, and aspirin to stop further blood clots. He was saved. He beat death, sat down at that eternal chessboard and played a winning game. The grim reaper wouldn't take him yet; wouldn't carry him away to elsewhere. But you knew that death was lurking somewhere, just around the corner, sharpened scythe swung up over one shoulder, black cape flapping like a vulture's wing.

My mother took it badly. She came back from the hospital pale, shaken, nerves frayed.

"He just looks *grey*," she said, and promptly burst into tears. "He lacks colour."

She fell into my father's arms and sobbed.

I didn't see my grandfather again until a year after the heart attack. I had been away at university, studying architecture, and was home for the summer. My parents and I went to pay 'the old folks' a visit. My grandfather sat quietly in his conservatory, looking out at the boats. He had always liked to watch them coming into the harbour; the ocean liners, the freighters, the sailing boats with their multi-coloured sails. He seemed altered, subdued, as if another piece of himself had been taken away - by the heart attack, or by something else. He'd smoked a pack a day for many years and now had emphysema. You could see him struggling for breath, labouring to get the air into his lungs, his shoulders rising and falling exaggeratedly as he inhaled and exhaled.

My grandmother was as chirpy as ever, full of beans. She'd made a pavlova in anticipation of our arrival. I had, by then, ditched the piano lessons and I evaded her questions regarding my musical education. I was busy with the course and with my new boyfriend, Luke; I had no time for chords major and minor, for notes flat and notes sharp. I felt that I could leave all that behind, shed my past as easily as a cicada shucking off its shell. Luke was a good looking guy; short dark hair, blue eyes, olive skin. He was reading Art History. For three months he walked past where I sat in the library six times a day, hands in his pockets, looking nonchalant until, eventually, I caught his eye and he plucked up the courage to ask me out.

Our first date involved him taking me back to his dorm room to show me his two axolotls; one male, one female.

"What are their names?" I asked.

"El Niño and La Niña," he replied. "Oceanic temperature fluctuations."

"Neat," I said. "Snappy."
They were albinos, their skin pale, almost translucent. The only way to tell them apart was that one's eyes were white, like snow, or a burning midday sun, while the other's peepers were pitch black, like the depth of the night. I knew those supposed opposites, knew them well – they were like the keys of those pianos that I once had played.

He had trained them. When he tapped on the side of the aquarium they would swim to the surface, anticipating food, the sliced little bits of kidney, liver and steak that he would give them once a day. Occasionally he would forget to feed them and they would start eating each other, gnaw at a leg or a gill, take a bite out of a tail – each other's, not their own. It didn't really matter that they munched at one another in this way, as they could grow back up to sixty percent of their bodies and thirty percent of their brains (not that anybody was devouring *those.*) A few times they'd had babies, and then promptly eaten them alive. Luke said that the axolotl was one of the most important evolutionary links, that this bizarre creature represented the borderline between fish and reptiles.

"If it weren't for the axolotl," he said, "and its ability to become something else, we might all still be swimming around in the ocean."

"Really?" I said. "What do they become?"

"Salamanders. If you take them out of the water, their gills will become lungs. But it's a very traumatic transformation, with a high risk of death, and to fully achieve metamorphosis, I think they usually need a shot of iodine or some sort of hormone. I wouldn't want to put the little buggers through it, to be honest. I mean, what for? My own entertainment? Just to see whether or not they make it – to place bets?"

"Oh, I agree," I replied. "You can't do that to them. They seem so happy where they are. Just swimming in little circles."

And they *did* seem happy, flapping round in that grubby little aquarium, their pink frilly gills floating out to either side of their heads.

"And once they evolve," I questioned. "Can they then go backwards? Can a salamander become an axolotl? Can lungs become gills?"

"Oh no," he said. "They can't *devolve.*"

"That's a shame, that there's no way back."

"Well, evolution, like time, is a trajectory, an arrow. A bullet fired from a gun. One way." Like most of the guys I was familiar with, he spoke as if he knew what he was talking about even when he didn't. It was a confidence trick; a way of fooling the world into thinking that you had become a man, when at least half of you remained stuck in boyhood. I wasn't sure that I agreed with him on the time issue, but I wasn't in any position to argue, since I had no solid evidence that time was not a line, only gut instinct, intuition. As I walked across the university grounds, I had felt weird blips, sensed loopholes, gaps in the space-time continuum. I lived on a knife edge; it was impossible to know what sort of apocalypse might be around the next corner. A hole in the ground could open up and engulf you. The sky might fall. The universe could throw an epileptic fit.

Did other people feel this way? In lectures, in the university café, in the dorm, I would scan their faces looking for signs; but they seemed oblivious, protected, safe. Were they not aware that the earth might be sucked into a black hole at any moment? When I expressed these fears to Luke he laughed and said that I worried too much.

"When your number's up, your number's up," he said.

"But what if *everybody's* number's up," I countered. "What if we're close to the end of the world – Judgement Day? What if it's all going to finish? What then?"

"There is no end," he said. "An end of *this* world would just be...the start of something else."

"Something else? What else? What if there's just nothing?"

"Errr...listen, I've got a lecture now. I'll meet you tonight at eight in the café at the end of King Street, okay?"

Nobody else seemed to appreciate the fragility of the human race, the precariousness of our position, stuck here, on this earth, just waiting for disaster to strike. God only knew what form it would take; could be hurricanes, floods, earthquakes, tidal waves, could be a plaque of locusts or a stray meteorite. Random acts of God. Whichever way you looked at it, we were a sitting duck. My parents, also, were oblivious to impending catastrophe, they didn't seem bothered – they were just as they had always been, keeping themselves busy, gardening, hiking, painting the weatherboards of our house. I had thought that my grandfather might have a clue, might know, but seeing him again, sitting in his cane chair in that conservatory, staring out through the glass, he seemed so far away, so distant. Whenever I tried to catch his eye he looked away.

Upon returning to university, I found that La Niña had died in my absence. Luke didn't get on with his parents, and he hadn't gone back home for the holidays. Instead, he had stayed on in the city, working on a construction site, saving some cash. Before I'd left for the summer break, we'd moved out of the dorms and found a place together. We were planning to cohabit. He'd come home from work one evening, to the new flat, to find La Niña floating upside down in the aquarium, while El Niño swam in melancholy circles around his dead mate. She was chewed, chewed badly. Luke had kept her strange little body in a shoebox and, on the first night of my return, he brought it out to show me, held her up to the light. Her corpse was dehydrated, shriveled, wizened. I held my nose - La Niña stank to high heaven. Large parts of her were missing; three legs, four gills, all of the tail. Clearly El Niño had taken more than sixty percent. "Hell," I said. "Looks like somebody got the munchies. Were you not feeding them properly?"
"Yea," he replied. "Every day. Plenty of meat."
But he muttered when he spoke, and kept his gaze fixed on the tips of his shoes.

Our flat was a run-down one bedroom affair on the top storey of an old apartment complex on the edge of the city, reachable only by a rickety set of stairs. The elevator had been busted for a decade. The walls were thin; at night I could hear somebody in the flat next door incessantly practising piano scales. They kept me awake right through the night. There was a dog, also, or a number of them, a pack - they howled at anything; the sun, the moon, casual passersby. The only compensation for the constant din was the view, which was extraordinary. On fine days we could see right across to the other side of the river.

I didn't sleep, that first term back at university. The dogs, the scales, Luke's snoring, all of it conspired to induce insomnia. Most evenings Luke wasn't home before ten pm; he said he was in the library, studying, he wanted to get First Class Honours. I would sit at the kitchen table, waiting for him to come home, playing the tabletop as if it was a piano, hands moving swiftly across the wood. My fingers remembered many tunes. But, of course, no music could ever come from a table.

The nights were not good, but the days were worse. I would switch off whenever the lecturer started talking about space and light, would fall asleep, awakening to find a pool of dribble on my paper. Looking around, I would see that everybody else had taken many pages of notes. In between lectures, I forced myself to study the structures designed by history's master architects; Frank Lloyd Wright, Adolf Loos, Denise Scott Brown. Their achievements seemed so phenomenal and they themselves so driven - as if it had been not merely buildings, but their very selves that they had been constructing.

Luke rapidly grew frustrated with my general malaise. "No matter what I do, no matter what I say, I just can't make you *happy*," he would declare, and I would shrug.

It was the truth - good point, well made. What did he want me to do about it? Wave a magic wand and cast a happy spell?

"There's just no pleasing you," he'd say and head down to the nearest pub, in a huff.

It was Easter. We were driving along back roads, on our way to a cottage that we had rented. It had been my suggestion, a selfish one. I had been hoping that country air and darkness and silence would help me to sleep. It was twilight. The headlights were dimmed. Luke was driving. He claimed later that he'd not seen the deer until it was too late to swerve or brake. It was as solid as a wall and hit the front bumper with a thud, like a bird in full flight colliding with a windowpane. It fell, we pulled over. It was still alive, still breathing. You could see its breath in the cold night air; like steam, like smoke. I was beside myself, or, as the French would say "out of myself" – I hated to see animals injured. The death of La Niña had been bad enough, but this felt like some sort of omen, some sign.

"Oh God," I said. "What are we going to do?"

Luke was silent – a rare occurrence. We stood for five minutes, watching the deer breathing, in, out, in, out, steady, like a heartbeat. No other cars passed us; the road was deserted, located as it was in the back of beyond.

The deer was down but not out. As we stood watching, it rose up, Lazarus-like, wobbled unsteadily and took a couple of tentative steps.

"She's fine," said Luke, and turned to me, smiling, as if the resurrection of the deer signified some sort of personal victory.

"How do you know it's female?" I asked.

"No antlers."

"But it's not yet winter. Maybe he's just not grown this year's antlers yet."

"Okay, okay. *It's* fine. God, I never can say the right thing with you."

The deer limped off into the forest, blended in, vanished, as if it had become one of the trees. In the instant before it disappeared, it turned and stared directly at me.

In the country, I slept the sleep of the dead. Ate large, hearty meals. Took long hikes alone through the forest, hoping in vain to see the deer. I never saw any trace of it, saw nothing; just heard the crows squawking in the branches and the rustling of the wind in the leaves. Luke stayed inside where it was warm, reading and watching TV. We didn't really talk. We didn't seem to have too much to say to one another.

I had spent so long anticipating an apocalypse that, when it arrived, it was almost a relief. I was sitting in the university cafe, drinking coffee to try and stay awake, when a tall, thin girl with long dark hair and bright blue eyes like Luke's sidled up to me. She pointed at the chair on the other side of the table, asked if she could sit down, said she had something she wanted to tell me. I knew it could only be bad news, but I agreed anyway, welcomed this harbinger of doom with open arms.

"Sure," I said. "Take a seat."

She sat.

"You're Luke's girlfriend, aren't you?"

"Yeah."

"Let me start by saying," she said. "That I really hate deception. You know, living a lie."

"Right. Me too."

"To cut to the chase, you know he's been seeing me, don't you. Every night – well, most nights. I gather he told you that he was studying."

I felt sick, like somebody had punched me in the stomach, yanked the carpet right out from under my feet.

"When you were away, he spent more time at my place than he did at his own."

The death of La Niña; the neglect I had suspected. I remained silent.

"Just thought you'd like to know," she said, before rising to her feet and leaving.

He didn't deny it.

"But I dumped her," he said. "Just last week. It's over."

"Hell hath no fury," I replied, as I packed the last of my belongings into my suitcase.

I didn't know whether I was talking about her or me. I took a taxi to the train station, caught a train to my parents' house. Where else could I go?

The second heart attack happened while I was howling at home. Another piece taken; something else claimed. While her husband was in the hospital, I went to stay with my grandmother. She didn't want to be alone. That first night, we sat together in the conservatory, watching the harbour lights. Her question came out of the blue.

"Why *did* you stop playing the piano?" she asked, after the two of us had sat in silence for a good five minutes.

I shrugged. I had no answer for her. Nothing to say.

My grandfather came home from hospital. I took the rest of the year off, tinkered on our old piano, wandered aimlessly around the neighbourhood, as if I was trying to find something that had been lost. I never knew what it was. At the start of the following year, I returned to university and resumed the architecture course; I was now a year behind everybody else. I lived with two other girls but kept myself to myself. Occasionally, I would see Luke in the distance, and scurry rapidly in the opposite direction. I couldn't afford a piano, so I didn't take lessons. I kept my nose to the grindstone.

But all this is in the past, and has no bearing on the present day.

Now I am supposedly an adult. People pay me to design their houses. I have my own piano, in tune, but I rarely play it. We gather now for my grandfather's eightieth birthday. My grandmother is fifteen years older than him - she used to call him her toy boy. She looks set to make a clean century. She keeps herself fit and active, plays mahjong, backgammon, golf. But he, he is fading, failing, on the way out. Everybody is here for this occasion; aunts, uncles, cousins, nieces, nephews. Everybody is wearing their best clothes. There are neatly wrapped gifts upon the living room table, and fairy lights strung up in the backyard, just waiting to be switched on. There is a pavlova in place of a birthday cake – it is spiked with unlit candles.

It is still light. We sit out in the garden, amongst the immaculately pruned roses, waiting for the birthday boy to grace us with his presence. He is upstairs, showering, dressing. Preparing himself. My father says that he thinks we should ask my grandfather if he ever killed a man.
"We need to know," he says.
*Before he dies*, is the thought that hangs in the air, unspoken. But me, I think that my grandfather should be allowed to take his secrets with him to his grave. After all, he fought for us, helped save us from being forced to join the Empire of the Sun. He could have died out there. Or worse.

There is good reason for it, the silence that returned soldiers keep.

## THE ORPHANS

There were three of them, the orphans; my father, his brother Clarence and his sister Heather. When my father was three, their mother died of cancer. A year later, their father, who was two decades older than his wife, followed suit. I live now halfway round the world from where I was born; such a long distance to travel. When I lived in that country I had no curiosity about the past - it held no intrigue. It was something inconsequential; it had been and gone and was no longer. It didn't affect me. But now that I am older and further away, I want to know. The seasons are reversed; a harsh London winter is a warm New Zealand summer. Last year I flew towards the sun, escaping the kind of grey that threatens to turn into something darker. In Auckland I stayed with Aunt Heather in her huge six-bedroom house, where I plied her with red wine and milked her for information about their upbringing.

"Oh, we ran wild," she said. "She wasn't much of a mother, our Mum. Even before she got sick she was in her room most of the time, curtains drawn, even on bright sunny days. I don't know what was wrong with her. They say that whatever doesn't kill you makes you stronger, but some people are broken by their lives. Just broken. Look at Brian Wilson."

Heather was a big Beach Boys fan. She knew every word to *Pet Sounds* and would sing along at the top of her lungs while she did the housework. She joked that she might get a sandpit installed in her living room, in homage to the great, crippled man.

The three children were adopted by their mother's brother, Edward, known to us all as 'Uncle Ed'. It must have come as a shock when, aged forty and childless, though married, he'd inherited three children, but he did well, loved them as best he could, fed and clothed and watered them and sent them off into the world. He lived to be ninety-five, dragging out the last five years of his life in a retirement village, refusing to leave his bed. He didn't dine at the table with the other residents, didn't partake of bingo or backgammon or any of the other games that were on offer, didn't attempt to converse with the many single woman who may have been interested in chatting with one of the home's few gents. Meals had to be brought to him where he lay. He gave up the ghost. The retirement village had been a last resort; my aunt had offered him the option of a nurse at home but he'd turned her down, insisting that he could take care of himself, even though he blatantly couldn't. He was as stubborn as a mule; when he complained of the cold, my aunt bought him two pairs of corduroys, telling him that they would keep him warm. 'Devil's fabric', he muttered, pushing the pants back into Heather's hands. She took him leftover spaghetti bolognaise; he gave one half-hearted sniff and declared 'Pasta, *blech*, foreign muck'. Over the years, his ways had set and hardened and they would not now be cast in a different mould. When they put him in the village, they found in his hall cupboard a huge stack of notebooks he'd kept in his old age.

"Notebooks," I said, when I heard about this find. "Really! What was in them?"

I was imagining Uncle Ed, hunched over a two-bar heater, pen gripped fiercely in hand, writing the story of his life, or inventing fabulous tales to entertain himself in his twilight years.

"Oh, I've got one here," said Heather. "Take a look."

I took the small book from her, pulled open the pages. The print was sprawling, like a drunk spider had dipped its legs in ink and gone scuttling across the paper.

"20 May 1996. Milk, 50c. Paper, $1.20. 21 May 1996. Dozen eggs, $2.10."

So, that was it, his masterpiece; a meticulous record of every last penny spent. A desperate semblance of order in a life with an ever-diminishing circumference.

On my bedroom wall there is a picture of my real grandparents. She doesn't appear sickly, my grandmother, instead she looks defiant, her chin jutting out at a jaunty angle, her hands clasped behind her back, as if she stands in a military line-up. She's a head shorter than my grandfather, who looks a lot like my father, only minus the beard - dark curly hair, big Jewish nose, thin lips. What could have affected her so much that she didn't want to get out of bed, thought life not worth living? What darkness could have dragged her down?

"Post-natal depression," said my aunt, taking a slug of her wine. "She was never the same after she had us kids." But how could Heather know for certain what her mother was like before children? She may have heard second-hand accounts from her father or other relatives, but these were only somebody else's version of the truth. Maybe her mother had always been fragile; her sadness lurking within like an alligator in a swamp, nostrils barely discernable above the water, just waiting for the ideal moment to surface. They frighten me, these relatives who gave in, who lay down and waited for death to claim them. I would prefer that they'd raged against the blackness, tried to find some smidgen of hope, but clearly they couldn't. For them, Pandora's box was empty. Their suns refused to shine and no other light could be found.

"It's late," I said. "Let's go to sleep and talk more tomorrow."

In the morning there was sun. It streamed through the windows and fell across the table where we sat eating breakfast, checking the paper to see what time the tide was in so we could go for a swim. Bees buzzed in the backyard. They sounded furious. They were my aunt's new hobby; her fridge was full of Tupperware containers that contained the golden comb. That's what we were eating, fresh honey on toast, glistening, sticky, when heavy footsteps came thudding down the corridor. *Stomp, stomp, stomp.* Heather had a student staying with her, a Chinese boy; Trevor was what he was called in this country, though he had another name as well.

"He did try to tell me his real name," said my aunt. "But I never could remember it, so we settled on Trevor. He's from the North of China, they're bigger up there. He's huge, wait till you see him. And the eating! Lord, the eating. He can put away ten large potatoes, no problem. Just shovels it in. Like a machine. He'll eat me out of house and home. But oh, he was in a terrible place before he came here. Ten of them in a four-bedroom house, living off dumplings and noodles, mice and ants everywhere. He's much better off here with me."

Trevor appeared in the doorway, a monolith of a man, well over six foot, with great broad shoulders and thighs like the columns of a building.

"Trevor, this is my niece Hilary. Hilary, Trevor."
Trevor nodded at me solemnly, sat down at the table, filled a large bowl with muesli and poured milk over it. He ate solidly, steadily, a man with an agenda. Head down, spoon moving from bowl to mouth, he slurped with appreciation. His hands were enormous. I tried not to stare.

"In China it's polite to slurp," hissed Heather, as we carried the dishes to the sink. "I haven't got the heart to tell him that it's different over here."

"You'd think that he might notice."

"Oh, I know. But he's in his own little world. Trevor!" she called out. "You coming for a swim?"

He nodded briskly and stomped back down the hallway to his room to get changed.

"Normally I take him to Point Chevalier," said Heather, "Where it's so flat you can swim straight out for miles and your feet will still touch the bottom if you try to stand up. But I think we'll go to Frenchman's Bay today, over in Titirangi, it's a nicer drive. It's been a while since you've seen some native forest."

The road looped and wound back on itself like a twisting snake. Trevor sat in the front, tapping his feet in time to *Caroline, No*, which blared out of the car speakers. The trees bent down their branches, dark green arms reaching towards the car. Houses nestled in amongst the hills, part of the landscape. You had to follow strict guidelines when you built here; they didn't want anything that was out of keeping or unsightly. Frenchman's Bay was small, secluded, with the obligatory pohutakawas dotted along the shoreline. Broken oyster shells lay scattered across the sand, glinting in the light, threatening to cut your feet as you walked across them. A few straggly looking hippies wandered along the road, eyes fixed on some vision invisible to mere mortals.

"Titirangi dreamers," said Heather. "They come out here for the seclusion and then they find that in the winter it rains almost constantly, and they move back into town."

Although it was mid-summer, the beach was steep and the water freezing. Heather and I dived straight in, and then swam back and forth, lapping the length of the beach. Trevor came behind us, waded in up to his waist, then dipped his head under and swam directly out, as if heading for the far side of the harbour.

I'd dragged myself from the water and was lying on my stomach, immersed in a copy of *The Mosquito Coast*, when I heard steps crunching towards me, felt somebody tap my shoulder. Behind me stood a middle-aged man in yellow Speedos with a pair of binoculars hanging around his neck.

"Is that your friend out there?" he asked, pointing to a small black dot that receded into the distance.

"It's a Chinese boy that stays with my Aunt," I replied.

"Oh dear," he said. "We have a lot of Asians drown out here. They're not used to the ocean. They only have rivers where they're from. This beach goes straight out to the harbour. If he gets caught in a riptide he's done for. It's best we send someone out to get him."

He ran down the beach to the lifeguard's shed. The speedboat was sent out, bouncing across the waves to where the dark head bobbed. Reaching his target, the lifeguard cut his motor, and motioned for Trevor to climb aboard, get in the boat. But Trevor was stubborn. He didn't want to lose face. He'd swum out on his own; on his own he would make his way back. He turned around and began heading for the shore, his breaststroke steady and determined, like his eating. Back he came, all the way, with the speedboat putting along beside him.

Heather was ready with the reprimand.

"Dangerous, Trevor," she said. "Very strong current. Oh, he's like you Hilary. Head-strong."

Trevor picked up his towel, dried himself off.

"Sorry," he said.

It was the first word I'd heard him speak.

"You were too far out Trevor. It's best to just swim up and down here."

She motioned the length of the beach.

"Not directly out to sea," she continued. "Oh, it's my fault. I should've told him. Come on then, let's get in the car. Clarence is expecting us later on this morning."

Having recently retired from his job in the health service, Uncle Clarence was working on the family tree. He'd traced it back to the late seventeenth century; now he'd come to something of a standstill, hit the point where ancestry fades into nothingness, or becomes so tangled that it's impossible to unravel. We sat at his living room table, looking out over the motorway that was being constructed in the near distance. Clarence had the family tree out and was using a ruler to point to various branches as he spoke.

"It gets a little murky in places," he said. "But some things are certain. We were Cockney Jews, we ran shops that sold fruit, veges, tobacco, various household items. Your grandfather lived round Whitechapel way as a boy, before he came out here. I'll give you the address and you can go pay the site a visit. We were from Israel originally, of course. If *The Da Vinci Code*'s to be believed, chances are that we're directly descended from Jesus."

"Oh Clarence," said Heather. "You and the bloody Da Vinci Code. Here, I brought you some honey."

She took a container full of comb honey from her handbag and put it on the table. He ignored her and kept talking.

"You've Spanish blood in you as well; Fernandez blood. That particular branch is a bugger to trace. There's so bloody many of them. Fernandez is the Spanish equivalent of Smith. One thing's certain though - Peter Dunway's got it all wrong. He didn't even pick up on the Spanish connection. Idiot."

Peter Dunway was a cousin who'd worked with Clarence in the heath service. He'd done his own family tree several years earlier and Clarence, who'd never liked him, who thought (rightly or wrongly) that Peter looked down his nose at him, was on a one-man mission to disprove Peter's version of our ancestry.

"Ridiculous," Clarence was saying. "He's way off track. God knows where he got his information from. He didn't back anything up, didn't provide any evidence. I've got the papers to prove that my tree's correct, boxes of documents out back, in the spare room. What's he got? Nothing. May as well have conjured his damned tree out of thin bloody air."

"Alright, calm down" said Heather. "Anyone for a cup of tea? Trevor, want to come and give me a hand?"

She headed for the kitchen and Trevor trotted after her, like a chicken following its mother round the yard.

"How's your Dad doing anyway?" asked Clarence. How's my little brother?"

"Yea, he's good. Just bought six new steers. They're called one, two, three, four, five and six."

The use of numbers for names had been my idea. The first year that he kept cattle, my father gave them affectionate monikers; Derek, Bertie, Spotty Face, Joe. When the truck from the abattoir came to take them away he was wretched, tears in his eyes, choking back sobs.

"You got too close to them, Dad," I said. "The names personalise them. You need to think of them as steaks in the making. Keep a decent distance between them and you."

In my mind I could hear him, calling out to them across the fields.

"One, one, one. Come on, one. Come on five. Come on boys, come on."

Even the use of the term 'boys' could be dangerous, could make the cows seem more like sons than animals, but he didn't cry the next time the truck came. He was tight-lipped, rigid; you could tell that he'd steeled himself internally. He was perfectly composed.

Heather returned with the tea.

"Here we are then," she said. "A nice refreshing cuppa. Come on Clarry, pull yourself away from that damned tree and talk about something else for a change."

Clarence stood up from his chair, gazed out the window.

"Bloody motorway," he said. "It'll ruin our view. And the *noise*. We'll have to get double-glazing put in."

He took a sip of his tea, sloshed the liquid back and forth through his teeth to cool it. Trevor followed suit, slurping noisily at his drink, into which he'd stirred three spoonfuls of sugar. But Clarence couldn't resist returning to his favourite topic. The truth was that he seemed to have little else to talk about.

"I'll post it to Peter when I'm done," he said. "Then he'll realise that you can't just decide on how the past was without backing up your claims."

"That's my brother," said Heather, "Putting the world to rights."

"It's not that the whole *world* is wrong. Just Peter Dunway."
From the look on her face it was obvious that Heather didn't believe a word he said. It *was* the world he was hoping to right; a world that wouldn't care what he said, what he did.

It was only after we left that I thought to ask about Clarence's wife.

"Oh, she's gone into hospital," said Heather. "She hasn't been at all well."

She tapped her forehead with one finger.

*I wish they all could be Californian*, sang Mr Wilson, weaving dreams of a golden land where the sun always shone; a fiction.

"That's just the way it is," my aunt continued. "Some of us swim, some of us drown. We know which team we're on, don't we Trevor?"

Trevor nodded, though I wasn't sure that he understood what Heather had said.

"Yes," he said. "We swim."

It was the most conversation I ever heard him make, and on the plane back to London I thought of it; Trevor swimming out into the bay, turning only when forced to and making it safely back to the shore.

# THE KILLING JAR

My son collects insects. The idea was planted in his mind when I took him to the Museum of Natural History and he saw how even the tiniest of creatures, with the most meagre of life spans, could have a chance to live forever. He stood thoughtfully before a cabinet that contained numerous prime specimens, all neatly labelled with both the Latin and the common names.

"They were killed by somebody a long time ago," he said. "And now they will never die. Isn't that right, Dad?"

"Yes Gerald, that's right."

I was listening with only half an ear. My mind was elsewhere. Relations between his mother and me had been a little fraught and I was thinking how best to protect him from our storms. I wanted to keep him safe. I wanted him to be happy. He tugged at my sleeve.

"Can I start a collection Dad? Can I please? Just a small one."

"Sure you can. I'll help. Come on, let's go get an ice-cream. I saw a Mr Whippy van parked up outside."

The Emperor of Ice Cream, lurking on every other street corner. I bought him a cone full of soft white mush, took his hand, lead him away from the museum. I'd thought that would be the end of the insect talk, but it turned out to be only the beginning.

Eleanor and I provided encouragement; we thought a hobby would be good for him. We let him use the garden shed as his workroom. For his tenth birthday I bought him a copy of Murray S. Upton's *Methods for Collecting, Preserving and Studying Insects and Allied Forms*. He memorised entire passages. I helped him prepare his tools of the trade; gave him a hand with the killing jar, the relaxing chamber, the spreading board. The killing jar was simple, just a basic preserving jar, into which we placed two inches of sawdust, before pouring over Plaster of Paris and allowing the mix to set, thereby creating an absorbent layer that was regularly soaked with nail polish remover. The little critters were knocked out instantly, humanely. The relaxing chamber, which prevented the insects from becoming too dry and brittle, was a plastic box in which sat a layer of sand that was moistened with water and rubbing alcohol. Across the top was a sheet of cardboard upon which you would place the insects that were in need of relaxation.

"Yea, chill out dudes," said Gerald, as he placed his first victims, a couple of lacewing moths and a small spider into his chamber. The spreading board was knocked together from balsa wood and glue. Good easy fun. Clean.

He wasn't fussy; any insect was a good insect to him. Shortly after he'd taken up his new hobby I overheard Eleanor on the phone to one of her friends.

"Oh yes," she was saying. "He'd pin and mount anything. Yes, he *does* take after his father."

Cockroaches, beetles, wasps, bees, grasshoppers, crickets, stick insects, butterflies, angel insects. The odd praying mantis. What had begun as a hobby had blossomed into an obsession. Nothing went to waste. The larger insects he pinned to cotton wool-coated cardboard before putting them in a frame. Some he gave away to startled friends and relatives, some he kept for himself. The smaller insects, or those otherwise unsuitable for pinning, were placed into a specimen cabinet that we picked up cheap from a garage sale. He was a neurotic labeller; nothing went unclassified. He'd learnt that at the museum, the importance of naming.

At first he was clumsy; there were numerous torn wings and split thoraxes, but within just a few weeks he'd mastered his art. He was swift, deft, deadly. From field to preserved state took less than twenty-four hours. One second you'd be happily flitting amongst the long grass, enjoying the warmth of the sun on your wings, the next you'd be snuffing it in his jar. His speciality was butterflies. To him there was no greater thrill than slamming his net down over those fluttering wings, capturing what had once been free. He was in love with the object; I was in love with the word. Entomology was his passion; etymology was mine.

I already knew a little about the word's origin, enough to know that nobody knows for certain where it comes from, though it's commonly assumed to stem from the notion that butterflies, or witches in that form, stole butter and milk. Online, I gleaned further random facts. The Greek word for butterfly was psyche, originally meaning 'soul' or 'breath', now meaning 'mind'. Is that what Gerald was catching, tiny minds? The Maori believe that the soul of a dead person comes back to the world as a butterfly. Was that what my son was framing on the wall - the souls of the dead?

It was after midnight when I took the call. The phone's ring awoke my wife, who switched on the table lamp, sat upright in bed and eyed me, hawk-like, as I spoke into the receiver. Even before she spoke, I knew who it was. Who else would call at that time of night?

"Hello."

"You promised me this wouldn't happen again. I was waiting for over an hour."

"Oh dear. Yes. Oh yes, I am sorry. That's terrible news."

"What?"

"I'm terribly sorry to hear that. Please, if there's anything I can do..."

"Yea there's something you can do. You can stay the hell away from me. It's over, Lawrence. Goodbye."

*Click.*

"Well?"

My wife raised an eyebrow.

"That was my cousin," I lied. "Her mother passed away last night."

"Cousin schmousin."

"You don't believe a word I say, do you?"

"I gave up believing years ago, Larry. I just wish you'd stop insulting me by spinning so much bullshit. A web of shit. That's what you've spun."

What was I supposed to say to that?

"Night then, dear. Sweet dreams."

Her reply was another *click,* the switching off of the light. I wasn't too worried by the phone call. My wife already knew what was going on – it was no great revelation to her.

"We stay together for Gerald," was what she told other people, though she must also have had her own private reasons for not leaving.

As for the other one, well, I knew from experience that she didn't mean a word she said. It had been over five times before.

Gerald's favourite place was the field behind our house; to him it was Elysian, paradisiacal. It was where he went to escape from Eleanor and me when we started arguing. Sometimes he returned with Tupperware containers full of creatures, sometimes he simply lay and watched his insect friends buzzing and feeding and mating, returned home empty-handed, having chosen to capture nothing.

It was late and we were in the middle of a blazing row when he found it. I don't recall now what we were arguing about, but we stopped short when he entered the house with a dark, scuttling shape in a clear plastic container.

"I've found something new," he said.

He was excited, a puppy with a fresh bone, salivating almost.

"Gerald!" exclaimed Eleanor. "I thought you were up in your room. What were you doing in the field at this time of night? It's freezing out there. You'll catch your death."

She held her hands to his cheeks.

"You need a hot shower," she said. "You need to warm up."

Gerald was too jubilant to feel the cold.

"Look," he said.

He peeled the lid of the Tupperware back a centimetre or so and we peered inside. It seemed nothing remarkable, an ordinary spider, just like all the other spiders he'd brought home. But to Gerald it was extraordinary, a miracle.

"I'll bet you anything you like," he said. "That nobody else has ever captured one quite like this."

At first we refused to believe him. It seemed impossible that something undiscovered could exist so close to home. We looked through all the literature, the many books on arachnids he'd withdrawn from the library, and searched extensively on that other web, the one spun in cyberspace. This exact spider was to be found nowhere, though we stumbled across photos of a few of its cousins.

"Looks like a wolf spider to me," Gerald said, with the air of an expert. "Lycosidae family."

*Thwack.*

With one swift swipe of a book he swatted dead a fly that was buzzing against the windowpane, and dropped it into the spider's lair. The spider stalked, leapt, snacked. "See how it pounces on its prey. It doesn't need a web to hunt. But look at those faint yellow markings. It's new, Dad. A new guy. You know what this means! I get to name it." I indulged him. If he was wrong, the world's biologists would soon put him to rights. *Pardosa geraldus* – the moniker he chose. PG for short. We published our findings in *BMC Evolutionary Biology*. Nobody protested, nobody said, 'I got here before you. This is not new.' It was official. The unknown had become known.

PG was placed in a special ice cream container that Gerald painted blue so that nobody would mistake it for garbage. We sliced holes in the lid. The container sat on top of the television, a sunny spot, a place for basking. Gerald joked that the spider seemed to improve our reception, especially when we turned to Channel Four, which was notoriously static-prone in our part of London. Sticks and leaves were provided by way of habitat; he was fed bugs that were captured especially for him. Sometimes I fancied that I could hear him shuffling about in his container at night, munching on sandflies, blades of grass stabbing at his body and legs, like tiny green blades. But that was only my imagination, a flight of fancy. Even a man with the hearing of a wolf would have been unable to hear such sounds, from where he lay, upstairs in his bed beside a wife full of muted fury.

A week later she called me at the university.
"Well?" she said.
Not even so much as a preliminary 'hello'.
"Well what?"
"Well what do you have to say for yourself?"
"Not a lot."
"Let me ask you this. Why did you even bother to arrange to meet if you weren't going to show up? Was it some kind of game? Yet another pathetic attempt to try and gain the upper hand? To assert your feeble manhood?"
"I forgot. It was Gerald's birthday."

"Don't *lie* to me."

"I have to go now."

"Yes, that's right. Run back to your words and their origins. You're doing the world such a big fucking service. That's *just* what the masses are crying out for; another tome from Lawrence E. Hopkins."

"I have to give a lecture."

"Well don't keep your loyal following waiting."

*Click.*

I know what I am to her - I am shades of grey, shifting sands. Unreliable. Treacherous. The truth is that if I left Eleanor to be with her she wouldn't want me; I would become boring, predictable, dull, soon to be discarded like last year's handbag. It's only because I am unattainable that she wants to attain me. From a distance, I glitter. Up close, I am muted, matt. I open up the gap between us and she falls right into it. Time and again, she falls right in. I extend a hand only to snatch it away when she reaches out to grasp it. She thinks I will fill some hole, some inner emptiness, but I only tear it open wider. To my wife, I am something different. To Eleanor I am rigid, stubborn.

"Everything's black and white to you, isn't it?" she asked once, rhetorically.

What she meant was that I am inflexible, narrow-minded, but I chose to take it as a compliment. Blackness absorbs everything. White light contains all colours.

After the lecture, I called her back and arranged to meet her that Sunday, in order to explain. You have to keep extending a bit of hope, or they get up and walk away from the chessboard. Hard to play against an absent opponent. She likes art galleries; I took her to the Tate Modern. She wore black, like a mourner at a funeral; a black pencil skirt, a black turtleneck, dark sunglasses that she kept on, even inside, where we looked at Cindy Sherman's self-portraits and rooms full of plain white boxes. Her red hair was slicked back in a neat bun. I held her hand, moved my thumb back and forth, as if to reassure her.

"I know it seems impossible," I said. "But please, hold on. I just need to wait until Gerald is old enough to leave home and then I'll leave too. I promise."

"I know your promises. They're fool's gold."

"If you won't wait for me, why should I continue to see you?" That's it, turn it around, throw it back onto her.

"You're fool's gold and I'm the world's greatest idiot," she said. But she didn't let go of my hand, even after we'd left the gallery and were wandering slowly towards the hotel.

I was in my study researching the origins of the word 'arachnid' when he knocked at my door. He entered before I could answer, came creeping in on cat feet, stood at my elbow.

"What's up love?"

"It's PG, dad. He seems angry."

"Angry? What does an angry spider look like?"

"He's pawing at the bottom of his container. Like this."

With his right arm he mimed a pawing action, snorted a little through his nose, like a bull about to charge.

"Oh dear. I see. And what do you think he's angry about?"

"He told me something."

"He *told* you something. Goodness. I didn't realise that you spoke spiderese."

"We have our own special language. Halfway between spiderese and human."

"Ah. You've reached a compromise. So what did he say?"

"Where were you today, Dad?"

"Today? I just went out for a bit. To meet a friend from university. You want Dad to have friends, don't you?"

"Yea, but…"

"But what?"

"Nothing."

"So, come on then. What did PG say?"

"He said that you had another girlfriend. Besides Mum. A different one."

"Now where would he have heard a silly thing like that?"

"He overheard Mum talking on the phone."

"Well, he must have misheard then, Trucker Boy, because Daddy only has one lady and that's your mother. Just one. There are no others."

"Stop calling me Trucker Boy, I hate that name."

"Okay then *Gerald*, he must have misheard."

"PG said that Mum said that you might leave us."

"Relax. I'm not going anywhere. Where would I go?" I held out my cheek for a kiss and he gave it a small, suspicious peck. He did not turn and walk away; instead he backed out the door. I could feel his eyes boring into me as I crouched over my computer, pretending to return to my work.

Three days later, further signs of trouble. White static on the TV screen; terrible reception. Rising from the sofa to tweak the antennae, I noticed that the lid of PG's container had been changed. An unpunctured black cover now kept him captive. How could he live through that? All God's creatures need oxygen. Gerald was upstairs in his room, playing Gran Turismo. I could hear the revving of computerised engines, the screech of digital tyres. I climbed the stairs, entered the room, stood right behind him. He didn't look round, just sat there with his eyes on the screen, making *vroom-vroom* noises as his body swung left and right with the movement of his car.

"Gerald! Did you change PG's lid?"

"Yea. He was getting bored of the old one."

"But there're no holes in it, Gerald. How's he supposed to breathe?"

"Oh yea, I forgot. Sorry."

He took a turn too fast, lost control, went skidding into a wall.

"Fuck!"

"Please don't swear in this house. Now where's his old lid? Let's put that one back on."

"I threw it in the bin."

"Gerald, honestly. Sometimes you just don't think."

"Yea whatever."

"If you can't take care of PG properly, he'll have to go back to the field."

"Oh high score!!"

A number flashed on the screen. He entered his name in the Hall of Fame, hit play, started a new game. I closed the door on my son and returned to the living room, where I removed PG's black lid and gave him a new, clear one, with sufficient slices in it. Then I went into my study to make a call.

I took her to the park. She likes parks. It was close to home, dangerous, I liked that. Had you climbed up onto the roof of our house you could have seen us, walking past the duck pond, which was beginning to ice over. Winter was drawing in. Most of the ducks had flown elsewhere, just a few hardy stragglers remained, huddled together, as if for warmth.
"So here we are again, then," she said. "The same old pattern, and neither of us brave enough to invent a new design."
"It's only a question of time," I replied.
"You're a stuck record."
"More like looptape, I think. Still, something's better than nothing, isn't it?"
She smiled a little, though it could have been a grimace. My right hand gripped her left elbow. I led her in amongst a small corpse of trees. Pulled her down into the dirt.

Eleanor was at yoga. She liked to stay supple, flexible. Sometimes I wondered if she wasn't having an affair herself – why else would she care so much about keeping in shape? It's not as if it was for my benefit. Gerald and I were sitting on the sofa watching *Big Brother*; fame decoupled from achievement.
"Spoke to PG again today Dad."
"Really? What did he say? I suppose he was angry with you for trying to suffocate him."
"Na, he's forgotten all about that. He told me something else."
"And what was that? What did the spider say?"
Any day now, I would tire of this game.
"He said he saw you in the park. Holding hands with a woman that wasn't Mum. A lady with red hair."
"Now how would he have seen that from his home? Can he see through walls?"
"He got bored and crawled out through one of the holes. Pulled it open with one leg. Went out for a bit of wander."

"Is that so?"

"He's got a lot of eyes, Dad. He sees things."

"So it would seem."

"He said you were having it off in the bushes."

"*Having it off?* Where did you learn that terrible expression?"

"From PG."

"Ah."

"I'm not saying it's true, Dad. I'm just repeating what I heard."

"Spoken like a true gossip. Listen, can two people play that Gran Turismo?"

"Yea. If they want."

"Come on then. I'll challenge you to a duel."

I put one arm around his shoulders and we headed up to his room where I let him beat me by a couple of laps.

Sunday morning. Eleanor busying herself in the kitchen. She liked us to breakfast as a family at the weekend - a semblance of togetherness. A hollow imitation of family life. Stepping out to fetch the newspaper; broken eggshells on the front doorstep, egg all down the door. My Ford Mondeo had also been targeted. I'd thought such petty, spiteful acts of vengeance were beneath her, but clearly I was mistaken. She'd always behaved with a certain level of dignity, but now the mask was slipping, the cracks were beginning to appear. Perhaps I was jumping to conclusions. It could have been somebody else. Neighbourhood kids skylarking about. Returning with a copy of *The Guardian*, I found Eleanor with the fridge door open.

"Where have all the eggs gone?" she asked. "Who's eaten all the eggs? I bought a fresh dozen just yesterday."

"Not me," I said.

"Gerald," she yelled up the stairs. "Gerald have you been into the eggs?"

"No Mum."

The distant drone of Gran Turismo, the soundtrack to our lives.

"I wish he'd quit playing that bloody game," said Eleanor. "Damn, I'll have to go to the shop. Make Gerald take a shower and come down and join us, would you?"

She put on some lipstick and collected her handbag from the sofa. I took a bucket and a sponge and cleaned up the mess.

A table for two at her favourite restaurant. She let me order for her, she's not good at making decisions, at least, not when she's with me. In her other life, her *real* life, she works as a lawyer in the city, a forceful, determined woman with a mind of her own. What I see is the other side, what she hides from those city boys, from her clients, from her small circle of friends. I am time out, time apart. A poisonous chink in her armour. Before the entrees arrived, I handed her the gift I'd bought to keep her happy, a single diamond, set in white gold, dangling from a thin chain. She gasped when she saw it, withdrew it from the box. It dangled from her fingers, sparkling in the light like a dangerous star.

"Oh, it's beautiful," she said.

"It suits you. Here, let me help you put it on."

I rose from my chair, stood behind her, draped the chain around her neck, fastened the clasp. Then I bent down low and whispered, "I just can't give you up."

Even to my own ears, the words sounded rehearsed.

"Like an addict returning for his fix," she replied. "If only there was a methadone program for what you're got."

That night I didn't go home at all; instead I stayed with her, in her austere apartment. It hadn't happened before.

"It won't happen again," I said to Eleanor when I returned at midday.

She stared at me icily.

"Go and look in the kitchen," she said.

On the table there was a pleasant surprise. *Pardosa geraldus*, dead in the killing jar, brought inside as gory evidence, as a cat would leave the gift of a slain mouse for its owner.

"Ever so *Fatal Attraction*," said Eleanor. "If you're going to fuck somebody, at least chose someone who won't come creeping round the house, murdering my son's pets. Well, goodbye PG."

She upended the jar and the spider slid into the bin.

"Where's Gerald?"

"Where do you think?"

In his usual place, hunched over the Playstation controls like a boy possessed.

"Gerald, did you know that PG was dead?"

"Course. I found him this morning. Out in the work shed."

"Why did you kill him? I thought you were proud of your discovery."

"I didn't kill him! He crept in there all by himself."

"Do you mean to tell me that he somehow escaped from his ice cream container, crawled all the way from the house to the shed and committed suicide?"

"I guess."

"Why would he go and do a thing like that?"

"He wasn't happy."

"Why wasn't he happy? He had a nice home and plenty to eat."

"I dunno Dad. Spiders aren't logical. Score. High*est* score!"

"Some people have to win, don't they?" said Eleanor.

She'd followed me up the stairs and had been listening at the door.

"Yes," I said. "Some people do."


It was only later, when challenging my son to another game of Gran Turismo, that I noticed that each time he won it was himself he was beating, for his was the only name that featured in that particular Hall of Fame.

## THE QUEEN OF GAYNDAH

We were both keen to leave the country we had been born in. Like all Commonwealth citizens aged twenty-eight or under, we had the right to live and work in Britain for two years. London was a super-highway; New Zealand, a dead end street. There was just one question – how best to earn the airfare and the two thousand pounds required for entry into the UK on a working holiday visa? The answer was simple. Fruit. Apples in New Zealand, oranges in Australia. Fruit seemed the answer to everything. We worked like demons. We were fitter than we'd ever been before. Bulging muscles protruded from our upper arms, as if small apples had lodged themselves under the skin. At night I dreamt of Granny Smiths, Pink Ladies, Braeburns; they swirled before my eyes like motes, the brain's mindless rehash of all it has processed during the day.

The best pickers on the orchard were Vicky and Sonia, whom Richard nicknamed 'the Superdykes'. They didn't mind the name they'd been given; they wore it like a badge of honour. Vicky and Sonia could pick half as much again as any of the men, filling their bins with ease. It was the Superdykes who told us about Gayndah, a small orange-growing town in Queensland. "You can earn good money. You'll be in London in no time." They seemed to know what they were talking about.

When the apple season finished in New Zealand, we bought ourselves two one-way tickets to London. The tickets included an Australian stopover. We flew into Brisbane, where we bought a second hand car. *Rust is just metal returning to its natural state*, one car salesman stated boldly, as if such a declaration would clinch the sale.

It was night when we pulled into Gayndah, but even in the darkness, you could tell that it was a no-horse town. Imaginary tumbleweed rolled down the main street.
"Turn the car around," I said. "We'll go to Sydney. I'll wait tables, work in a café. It'll take longer to get to London, but I don't care."
Richard was not so easily deterred.
"Come on," he said. "We're here now. Let's just try and stick it out for a bit. Give it a month."

That first night was spent in a cramped room above a pub. In the morning we would look for a more permanent place to stay.

Enter Nita. She ran the largest campground in the town and was the employment officer for the region. Nita was Dutch, she'd come over from Holland in the sixties and established herself as a local figure, authoritarian, a heavyweight. Her hair was a curious shade of pink. If she wanted you to work, you worked. Conversely, if you got her back up, you would find yourself sitting around twiddling your thumbs until you gave up and went elsewhere. She liked to think that her condemnation was the equivalent of "You'll never work in Hollywood again" though personally, to have heard her utter "You'll never pick fruit in Gayndah again" would have been a less than crushing blow. Her caravans weren't cheap; a hundred bucks a week. Her favourite quote was, "I'm the most powerful woman in Gayndah." It was quite a boast – during the height of the orange season Gayndah had about three thousand residents; the rest of the year, the population dwindled to around five hundred. We named her campground 'Nita's Place' and Nita herself 'Queen of Gayndah'. The Superdykes had arrived at Nita's Place a week before us. Sonia had her son Kane in tow, a hard-working boy, half-Maori, aged about eighteen. Shortly after I'd been introduced to Kane, I was in the campground office buying some two-minute noodles, when I overheard Nita on the phone. She mentioned Kane's name, (presumably to a potential employer) then said, "He's coloured, you know." I didn't tell the others what I had heard.

Nita found us a job working for 'Crazy John' who may well have been the sanest person in the entire town. John was deaf in one ear, and sang loudly and atonally to himself as he made his way amongst the trees. A decade previously he'd been beaten senseless by a local gang and left for dead under a bridge. He'd been in a coma for three months. Now he lived with his father in their small three-bedroom cottage and only left the orchard when forced to go out for supplies.

"Cops didn't give a shit," John's father told us, wandering out to talk to us once day, as we sat taking a tea break amongst the trees. "Word was that one of them was involved in the beating. Animals."

He spat on the ground then scuffed at the spit with his brown leather boot. A large spider went scuttling by and he stomped it flat, eight spindly legs squished against the dirt. All the insects seemed larger here. There were Huntsman spiders whose circumference was that of a small coffee cup – they nestled in amongst the oranges and crawled up your arms and across the back of your neck when you snipped the fruit from the trees. A Huntsman wouldn't kill you, its venom was hardly even toxic, but the feel of spider legs scuttling across skin inspires an instinctive repulsion. First day on the job, I saw an enormous spider web spun in the leaves of a high branch with a frog skeleton suspended in it. The spider was nowhere to be seen; like the shark in Jaws, it was all the more frightening for its absence. If that was the size of the prey, how big was the predator?

Once you've ruled out your immediate cousins, decent wives are hard to come by when you live in the back of beyond. The petrol station we frequented was run by a short, fat, balding guy with a mean face and scarred hands. I'd ask for a coffee and he'd yell, "Fifi! Fifi, get downstairs and make this girl a hot drink!" The young woman that we took to calling 'the bride' would tiptoe down the stairs, rubbing the sleep from her eyes, and creep quietly to the counter. She was always in her nightgown. She was tiny, barely five foot, and thin, like a twig you could all too easily snap. Her skin was a dark shade of olive. She caught nobody's eye, as she shuffled about behind the counter, spooning Nescafé into a polystyrene cup, pointing silently to the milk and sugar, handing me a small wooden stirring stick. When done, she would head back up the stairs, leaving her husband to deal with the financial transaction. She steered well away from her 'other half' – flinching if he came near her, the expression on her face like that of a caged animal, or a dog that's been all too regularly beaten.

I began to feel almost guilty about asking for coffee – it was always early when we arrived, six-thirty a.m., and it was obvious that I was dragging the poor woman out of bed. On other mornings we would call in at the small café in the centre of the town, but it seemed to make sense, when filling up the car, to get my caffeine fix at the same time. There was nowhere in the town to get real coffee; Nescafé was as good as it got.

"Where do you think she's from?" I asked Richard, the first time that I laid eyes on the bride.

"Dunno. The Philippines? She's definitely mail order. She ain't from round here," he added, mimicking a Southern drawl.

"Fifi can't be her real name though."

"No. It's probably just the name he gave her. Has a kind of cheap porn star ring to it, no?"

There were plenty of them out there in Queensland, women ordered online, or from a catalogue, packaged up and shipped over. Fresh meat. How much were they paid to leave behind their old lives and head blindly off into the unknown? Nothing probably, they'd been enticed by the offer of a new existence, a better life. To even consider such a marriage seemed an act of pure desperation. No doubt the bride had been sold grand dreams, dreams that would have turned to nightmares when she realised what she'd bought into. What overblown promises must have lured her to this country; what disappointment must have flooded through her blood when she arrived, when she awoke to find herself married to a heartless thug. It wasn't hard to imagine what she'd left behind; a cramped, cockroach-infested apartment, crammed with too many relatives, a bleak future filled with monotonous labour or prostitution. Australia must have seemed like a land of plenty, full of wide open spaces and kind-hearted, sunny people with relaxed, easy-going lifestyles. Endless barbeques, a swimming pool in every backyard. Long summer evenings sitting out on the porch. Now she cowered upstairs like the madwoman in the attic. Her husband probably tore up the letters that her family wrote; mail never received.

One morning she came to the counter sporting a black eye; the following week she had her arm in a sling.

"Don't you think we should say something?" I asked Richard, when we returned to the car. "Tell the police."

"They won't care," he said. "This is Hicksville. *Deliverance* territory. Domestic abuse is overlooked out here. They turn a blind eye. Your woman is yours to do what you want with. A possession. A chattle.

To have, to hold and to smack senseless on a Saturday night."

For better or for worse.

Wife-beating may well have been the norm amongst many of Gayndah's couples, but when it came to Nita and Bert there was no doubt as to who wore the pants. Nita ruled both Bert and the campground with an iron rod. She had rules, the weirdest of which was the 'No Grouping' rule. Grouping was defined as a gathering of more than two people in any given place at any given time after eight p.m. If she caught you 'grouping', she would send Bert over to break it up.

"Bert!" she would screech, her voice like a car alarm. "Bert, these people are *grouping!*"

She pronounced it 'glooping'.

"Over there, Bert, third caravan from the corner. Sitting outside at that little white table."

Off Bert would go, loping across the campsite, *okay guys, break it up, break it up.*

"But we aren't doing anything! We're just sitting out here talking and drinking a couple of beers."

"You're *grouping.* The rules were explained to you when you arrived."

"Yeah, but we thought you were just kidding. We didn't realise this was a rule that you were actually intending to *enforce.*"

"Rules are rules."

"Well, this one's a crazy fucking rule. What happens if we don't obey?"

"Then you will have to leave."

There was no choice but to do as the man said; Nita's was the only campsite that had any caravans left. At this time of year, space was at a premium.

"Forget deep South," Richard muttered. "This is more Third Reich."

Nita was egalitarian in administering her laws. Nobody was exempt. One fine summer evening, four retired Brits who were touring the country in their hired campervan pulled into the campground. They cooked and ate dinner and then, as the sky grew dusky, settled down outside for a nice game of bridge. Fatal error. The grouping alarm went off, the enforcer was sent, the lawbreakers were hurried inside.

"Can we play bridge indoors?"

"No. Nine pm. Lights out. Lie down. Keep quiet. Keep still."

London during the blitz.

Mockery – the last refuge of the oppressed. Kane bought paper and a red felt-tipped pen from the local stationery shop and made several 'No Grouping' signs (stick figures inside a red circle with a diagonal line struck through it). When Nita and Bert had gone to bed, he stuck the posters to the toilet block walls. It was a harmless gesture, albeit of the two-fingered variety. By morning all the signs had been taken down.

Gayndah was a place that nobody seemed to leave. The residents liked it there, they felt safe. Unlike Richard and me, they were content to die where they had been born. The world beyond was threatening, vague storms hung on distant horizons. The world was vicious and cruel; it would eat you alive. Every now and then some rash young upstart would fail to heed the warnings of friends and family, and head off to Bundaberg (*Bundy*) chasing some job building boats, or in the rum or ginger beer industry. Within a week, they'd be back, cloaked in defeat.

"Yeah, you were right all along," they'd say. "I didn't think much of the city, either. It's much better back here. All my mates just down the street. What more could you want?"

It was as if all those roads that appeared to lead out of town actually looped back on themselves and brought you right back to where you had started from. The nearest city was Brisbane.

"Went to Brissy once, didn't think much of it. Too many people, everyone busy-busy. Rushing to get nowhere if you ask me."

Political correctness had failed to reach this neck of the woods. Women were 'sheilas' and aborigines were 'coons'. The few aborigines who lived here were broken, destitute, alcoholic - Australia's untouchables. The whites ignored them, just passed right by without so much as a glance, as if they were non-people, invisible, as if they didn't exist at all. Not so much marginalised as pushed off the edge of the page, herded up and driven over some cliff, as was done to their Tasmanian kindred.

For me, the library was the town highlight. It was run by Ellen, a little old lady who drove a big old Holden. She could barely see over the steering wheel. Ellen was a gem; she would order you any book you wanted. On the shelves I found *The Obstacle Course* and *Millroy the Magician*, no doubt requested by pickers before me. I couldn't imagine any of the locals desiring such books, but perhaps that was presumptuous of me. The other main source of literature was the town paper. It consisted of ten pages filled with riveting articles; local news for local people. *Whitson's Ewe Gives Birth to Twins*, read one headline, with an accompanying photo that showed a sheep and her two offspring posing for the camera, daffodils springing gaily at their feet. *Anne Tariff Returns From Dentistry School. Welcome Back Anne. Anne will take up residence as a dental assistant at Gayndah Dental Care. Please call in and say hi.*

Friday nights were spent at Davo's Steakhouse; ten bucks got you a barbequed steak as big as a dinner plate and as many vegetables as you could eat. There were nasty rumours in circulation about Dave buggering one of his male staff with a broom handle one dark and drunken night, but we didn't like to think about that, as we drank Dave's beer and chewed the tasty steak he served up.

And once a week, the bride, shuffling about like the aborigines – another spectre. I wanted to say something to her, to extend a hand, but what could be said, given the circumstances? *Find your way back home. What could be worse than this living death?* I told myself that she was secretly happy, somewhere within; dancing on the inside. I lied.

In the end, we were evicted from Nita's place for sharing a pork roast. She smelt it cooking and came to investigate. She had the nose of a bloodhound.
"What's going on in here?" she questioned, ascending the three small stairs that lead inside.
"Just cooking up a bit of pork," replied Richard.
Nita pulled open the oven.
"That's a very big roast for two people."
"We thought we'd share it," said Richard, gesturing towards the two other caravans in which our friends stayed.

"Share?" she said. "*Share?* Well, you can't eat together. You can't gloop."

She checked her watch.

"It'll be well after eight by the time that thing's cooked."

"Oh no, no," Richard reassured her. "We wouldn't dream of *glooping.* I thought I'd just dish it up on plates and take it over, then run back here to have ours."

She eyed him suspiciously, said nothing, backed out the door.

When the roast was cooked, we snuck the food into a backpack and carried it over to sit with the others, cracked open a couple of bottles of wine and a tin of apple sauce. The huntress waited to pounce. As we were clinking glasses and saying 'chin-chin' she came bursting through the door. She was livid. Her face had gone pink and matched her hair. For once, she hadn't sent Bert to do her dirty work.

"This is an outrage," she shouted. (*Outlage.*) "Flaunting my laws. This is my campground and I make the rules (*lules*). Out, all of you, out by eight am tomorrow."

Kane was filming her on his new digital camera. Later, we watched the footage, crippled with laughter. Nita's rage seemed rehearsed, as if she was acting out some comedic role the director had allocated to her, a role she played without understanding or heart.

The incident was our cue to depart for London. We'd saved enough money. We were good to go.

We set out early the following morning, calling in at our usual petrol station to fill up the car. One last cup of coffee for the road. This time our tattooed man did not call up the stairs, but made my Nescafé himself, pushed it grudgingly towards me.

"Where's your wife?" Richard asked.

"Gone back home," came the mumbled reply.

That was his story, but on the way out of town we stopped in to say goodbye to John and his father and they told us the truth.

## MANDY

All men have a secret love. In the rose garden of declared desires, public passions, acknowledged amore, there lies always a hidden clover, an infatuation concealed from the world. A love that dare not speak its name. A love that has no name. An obsession. Mandy was mine.

Her limbs so long, lithe and elegant. The contradictions in her nature; her predilection for prayer combined with the sense that, just beneath the surface of such devoutness, lurked the dark power of the femme fatale. The long neck that seemed to turn almost backwards to watch me whenever I tried to creep up behind her. The round eyes that saw everything, saw me. Perfect. When I first found her, I bent down low and whispered in her ear, "Darling, how I long for you to rise above. How I long to see you fly."

Oh, the way she would look at me when I walked in the room, as if I were nothing more than an intruder in her immaculate world, as if she would never deign to venture this side of the glass pane that separated her from me. The way she would so nonchalantly shuck off her old skin to become somebody new. The way she liked her crickets still chirping.

I remember the first time she shed her skin, how I watched, quivering, as she sidled up to the nearest rough surface, secreted the glue that would hold her old self to the bark, then began to chew at the encasing that had once held her together, but that now threatened to hold her back. A small hole, a tear at the top of the thorax, then the struggle; the wriggling and the jiggling. How I cheered as she burst free! Had you seen my face that day, the day of the first shedding, you would have thought she was the first female in the history of her species to achieve such emancipation. We celebrated together, me with a glass of fine champagne, and she with a small newt I had thrown her way as a special treat. My honey, my carnivore.

I raised her from a nymph. She had been abandoned; her mother dead or flown the coop, and she, all alone in my backyard, barely out of the egg sack. An innocent. Green. When I found her she was alone, so alone, barely half a centimetre in length, and wingless. I snapped off the twig on which she perched and hurried her inside, least she be eaten by a foreign predator or, cannibalistically, by one of her own kind. Her home was a large preserving jar into which I placed an arrangement of sticks and leaves. For her I trapped small insects, midges, flies, moths, and dropped them, live, into her chamber. She liked her meat still kicking. A sliver of an ox's heart was used to attract her food; it sat in an ice-cream container on my kitchen bench, stinking. With my bare hands I caught the odd cricket. She was both my captor and my captured, both my jailor and my prisoner.

How can a man love what he doesn't understand? No entomologist myself, were she and I to cohabit happily, I knew that I would have to do some serious research. The day after finding her, I found myself lounging in a comfortable chair in the university library, engrossed in a copy of *Entomology Today*, within which I had found a fascinating article on the myths surrounding the mantis, whose name, I discovered, was derived from the Greek word for diviner or prophet. I learned that in France it was thought that a praying mantis would point a lost child the way home, in Arab cultures it was believed that the insect prayed facing Mecca, and in Africa, not only were the creatures thought to bring good luck to whomever they landed on, but they were even believed to hold the power of restoring life to the dead. In the United States, they had the idea that the mantis was evil, that the creature could blind men and kill horses, whereas in China, roasted mantis eggs were fed to children as a supposed cure for bedwetting. Such myriad powers! A woman's voice spoke my name.
"Dr Raprey?"
I turned to see a vision in shimmering green silk standing beside me, a tall young woman, well over six feet, and thin, like somebody who had been stretched at the rack. Her eyes sat prominent and slanting upon her face, which was all sharp angles, like a Picasso painting. Her skin was a light olive shade and her thick dark hair hung down about her face. Was she part Asian? She sat down in the chair opposite me and arranged her long limbs. Her bulbous eyes fixed themselves upon me; I was a rabbit caught in the glare of the headlights of an oncoming truck.

I held the magazine more closely to my face, in an effort to pretend I hadn't seen her, but she snatched the literature from me, threw it upon the small table that sat between us and pushed several sheets of paper into my hands, an essay. "B plus," she snarled loudly, oblivious to the *No Talking* and *Please Be Quiet* signs that adorned the library walls. "Do you realise, Dr Raprey, that never before in my life have I received such a lowly grade? Why, it's barely above average, is it? Pathetic."

I recognised the title - *The Borderline: the Divide between the Human and the Animal in Postmodern Fiction.* This was something I had marked, late at night, barely paying attention to the contents, just skim reading really, handing out the grade I gave when I couldn't be bothered making a decision as to the quality of the paper, an inoffensive sort of rating. So I had thought.

"Well," I whispered. "B plus is really a pretty good grade. Are you in the Honours programme?"

"Of course I'm in the Honours programme," she said, obviously offended.

"Maybe we should discuss this elsewhere," I hissed, only too aware of the angry looks we were attracting.

"Sure," she said huffily, rising to her feet. "Where do you suggest?"

I took her to a small café nearby where I bought her some lunch. I promised that I would read the essay again myself, and then get it checked by the Head of Department. She seemed satisfied with that, and certainly during our little exchange she seemed to have worked up quite an appetite, for although it had barely gone midday, she ordered a mixed grill, and attacked the chops and sausages with relish, impaling her knife into the flesh as if she feared the meat might escape from her plate. I watched, fascinated, barely touching the salad sandwich I had ordered for myself.

"What's up with you, goggle eyes?" she asked, when she was close to completion, and, surely, to satiation. "Don't you know it's rude to stare?"

"Alright," I said. "Don't bite my head off. I'm just intrigued at how you can polish off so much for lunch and still be so thin."

"Ever met a lady who was six foot three before?"

"Well, no."

"There you go then. There's a lot of me to feed. Hollow legs." When she had finished, leaving on her plate nothing but the chop bones and the odd fatty piece of gristle, she dabbed her mouth daintily with her napkin, a gesture very much at odds with the manner in which she had polished off her meal. I started in on my sandwich, feeling strangely fearful, as I had in my head the odd notion that, despite the quantity of meat she had consumed, she remained unsatisfied. She watched me finish eating, then excused herself, and rose to make her way to the Ladies' room. As she walked away, I noticed for the first time how the silk dress she wore was not just the one shade, but many, a sort of technicolour dream dress. It was the girl's surroundings that seemed to bring out the different tones in her attire; here, in the café, it seemed more a creamy colour, almost neutral. In fact, as she got further away from me, it became very difficult to see her at all, so successfully did she blend into the background. I could have sworn that, in the library, the dress had been green, and matched the walls there, but as I saw her step in front of the red door that marked the entrance to the Ladies' room, I watched her garment change gently, slowly, almost imperceptibly, from cream to red. I checked again the cover sheet of the essay, in order to give a name to this creature. *Amanda Beaufort*, I mused. *Strange goddess.*

Back in the safety of my office, I noticed that I had unwittingly stolen the magazine I had been browsing in the library. I leant back in my leather chair and engrossed myself in the ways of the mantis. Preyed on by birds, bats, spiders and snakes, the primary defence mechanism of my clever pet was camouflage. Masters in the art of mimicry, various types of mantis have been known to mimic flowers, or, as nymphs, ants. She could become whatever she wanted to be. If blending in failed, all was not lost. She had a range of other defence mechanisms, aggressive displays, such as rearing onto her hind legs and raising her menacing forelegs to expose false eyespots on the thorax that can confuse a predator, or rearing up and rattling her wings to create a hissing noise intended to intimidate those who wished to do her harm.

The more I read about her, the more she fascinated me. It seemed to me that the mantis was not a creature less, but more highly evolved than the human; an angel come to earth in insect form. I loved her for the variety and splendour of her defensive techniques, but also for her vulnerability. For if it all failed, the camouflage, the intimidation, she would be left defenceless, without caustic acids or toxic chemicals to ward off attackers, her cumbersome proportions now a hindrance, this earthbound misfit would make a good meal.

She was both predator and prey. The more cynical would say the only thing mantids seem to pray for is a square meal, but they didn't know her like I did. It's true; she was a hungry girl. Her kind ate mostly insects and other arthropods, but they were not adverse to munching vertebrates. They would eat animals larger than themselves; small lizards, frogs, snakes, and mice have fallen victim and, in one well documented case, a hummingbird was caught by a mantis, only to be freed by human intervention. Despite the voracious appetite of her species, I still felt that her praying position was more meaningful than just lying and waiting for the next victim. Surely she was deeper than that.

I stumbled across her again as I was walking past the church on King Street the following morning. There she was, as still as the stone steps on which she sat, reading, of all things, a copy of the New Testament. The pages were not turning, and no part of her moved as she read, not even her eyes.
"Amanda?"
It felt strangely improper, speaking her name like that, so out in the open, as if the socially correct thing to do would have been to ignore her and go about my business.
"Dr Raprey!" she said, springing to her feet in a single swift movement. "I was wondering if you would be coming by. I've often seen you walking this way in the mornings."
She'd been observing me, studying my patterns, my habits, when I had fancied myself invisible to the female gender, a neutered

shadow, going about my day to day routine, not bothering anybody and not expecting anybody to bother me. She made me uneasy; she seemed determined to catch me off guard.

I had her essay re-marked and raised the grade from a B plus to an A minus; she accepted this somewhat reluctantly, waving her arms about as she explained to me the pressure she was under to keep up an A average in order to secure herself First Class Honours. We struck up a strange kind of friendship that consisted primarily of her lying in wait for me outside lecture theatres, or on the steps of the church, and then springing out and accosting me as I walked past. We would sometimes have lunch together, she devouring a plate of meat and me picking half-heartedly at some sort of salad. Very few words passed between us, and yet we seemed to have an understanding; we were outsiders, peripheral, misfits. I noticed that she was always alone; I never once saw her mixing with the other students, sitting in the Union building enjoying a coffee, or stretched out on the lawn in the summer, and I, for my part, limited my conversations with colleagues to a brief chat around the water cooler. I never was much of a people person. In contrast to my innate scruffiness, she was always well dressed, often in silk and always in earthy tones, browns and greens and shades of grey.

The months passed by uneventfully, with my pet and Amanda my only two sources of company.

Having always thought of her as a solitary creature, when I saw them together, the physical reaction I experienced was of such intensity, that I ran to the nearest toilet to vomit. He was far taller than I was, with broad shoulders and fair hair. They were sitting in the university café holding hands. She was gazing at him as if all the secrets of the universe were etched upon his features. I was, as usual, on the other side of the glass; an outsider looking in. I'd assumed we had an understanding, she and I, we were different, unique. And here she was, throwing her head back and laughing. Mocking me. I felt bereft, betrayed.

I successfully avoided her for days. It was easy enough for me to hide. I simply shut myself in my office and locked the door. On more than one occasion, I fancied that I heard her knocking, but when I peered through the keyhole, it was never her standing on the other side, it was always some spotty-faced first year, and I never opened up. The first week after the sighting, I missed half my lectures, and sometime during the second week, I gave up altogether on going in – I called in sick every day. I sought solace in the true object of my affections, who was beginning to blossom. I knew it wouldn't be long until my darling craved a mate. Both of us were in need of a distraction.

It seemed that she had grown so quickly, seemed like just yesterday when I had found her in the yard, and here I was, already caught up in tomorrow, forcing myself out of the house, scurrying to the local pet shop, hoping to buy her a man.
"Awright darlin'?" greeted the woman behind the counter as I walked in. "Can I help you with something?"
I sidled up to the counter and lowered my voice.
"I was wondering if you had any...any..."
"Yea? What?"
"Any male mantids."
"Sure we have love. Dozens. All in separate tanks. They eat each other otherwise. Right this way."
I followed her to a back room where, against one wall, were a row of small glass enclosures, within each of which perched a male mantis.
"Which one takes ya fancy?" asked this madam. "What about number nine?"
She pointed at the ninth cell in the block.
"Yea sure. He looks fine. Is he old enough? Has he, you know...come of age?"
"Yup, he's legal alright," she replied, grinning up at me with nicotine-stained teeth as she took the mantis from his home and placed him in an old ice cream container.
"That'll be five bucks. Good luck."

She winked at me slyly, as if she knew some secret I didn't, as if she were a sorcerer, and I, her unwitting apprentice. I paid up the money and walked quickly home.

She'd not had any breakfast and was no doubt feeling rather peckish. I lowered her potential mate gently into the aquarium. He began to dance about a bit, waving his antennae and moving his abdomen in a figure-eight pattern. She eyed him up, he moved closer, she didn't resist. I ran upstairs to get my camera and when I came back down, things had obviously been a little gruesome in my absence, for he was nothing more than a body, a body that continued its act; the headless humper. I clicked away on my camera. After the body had finished its grim task, she consumed that also. I cannot say I was sorry to see him go, my competitor in the race for her affections, although I felt a slight guilt, for I knew that, had I fed her before mating, her man might still be alive. Still, nature was cruel, and who was I to play God?

After Mandy's first mating, I felt a lot more positive about life. The dark clouds that had hung about me since seeing Amanda holding hands with another man lifted, and I was able to return to the university feeling, if not exactly buoyant, at least a little less leaden. The institution was abuzz with the news. There had been an accident, a tragedy of sorts. A gifted student cut down in his prime in the most unusual of ways – he had been riding a train with a friend, they'd been larking about with their heads out the window, when the train had entered a tunnel, and, whilst the friend had pulled his head back in time, our poor medical student had not, and had been cleanly decapitated.

"Can you believe it?" a colleague asked me rhetorically. "It's the stuff that nightmares are made of. And just when he'd become engaged to that girl, the one I used to see you with occasionally. The tall skinny one."

She tracked me down in my lair; no doubt she sought comfort. Down on my knees, squinting through the keyhole, I could see her there, on the other side, as refined and as elegant as ever, dressed, for once, in black and wearing dark glasses. But I'd tired of her by then, as we will tend to tire of the things we thought we wanted, when they present themselves to us. I didn't see why I should open up now and let her in, not after the damage she'd done.

That night I caught a small frog for Mandy and placed it gently inside her jar. It was supposed to be a celebration, but it wound up a catastrophe. There was a battle, a terrible battle and I cannot bring myself to tell you who won and who lost. Suffice to say, there was just the one victor, and that I went to bed that night the owner of an altogether different sort of pet. It was an outcome I could never have foreseen. For how was I to know, when I placed the frog in her jar, who owned the greater hunger, who would be devoured, and who emerge alive?

# THE NEW HEART

The memories started six weeks after Tom Davidson had been given his new heart. The operation had been a success; Gerald Morton's ticker beat in his chest as easily, as freely, as if it had always been there, as if he, Tom, had been born with it. The doctor had discharged him from the hospital, telling him to take it easy for the first month, but he didn't feel like relaxing, he felt like climbing mountains, running marathons, belting songs from the rooftop. Was this what they meant by a new lease of life? He felt incredible, all-powerful, omniscient, like a god. It swelled, this new heart, it wanted to burst from his chest and scatter across the universe. Against his wife Kathleen's advice, he quit his job as a used car salesman, the job at which he'd excelled for the last twenty-five years, bought himself a mountain bike and started going on sixty-mile bike rides. Although he'd never skied, he purchased a pair of new Salomons and booked a ticket to St Anton, went sliding down the slopes, helter-skelter, barely even bothering to turn or snow-plough, just pointing his feet straight down the learner's slope and hoping for the best. He wrote poetry for his wife, left little love poems scattered about the house, like a cat leaving gifts of dead mice for its owner. Kathleen shook her head, scrunched up the notes, threw them in the bin. Then the memories started up. The first was of a girl, a freckle-spattered redhead with skin so pale you could see the veins through it. She sat on a swing, he was pushing her, her legs rose and fell, she looked back over her shoulder and smiled, so pretty in the evening light. She was no-one that Tom had ever known. She was Gerald's younger sister.

He kept a photo of his donor on the mantelpiece. Gerald Morton had been a twenty-five-year-old sports enthusiast, employed by Cannon's gym as a personal trainer. He'd harboured a passion for literature; had shelves full of Milton and Dickens and Shakespeare. Wallace Stevens. *The Norton Anthology of Modern Poetry.* Mr Davidson knew all this because, after the memory had appeared, he went to visit Gerald's mother. Mrs Morton spoke proudly of her son, his passions, his interests and of the tragedy that was the car crash that had taken his life. She

read him her son's favourite poem; *The Well Dressed Man With a Beard.*
"I'm so happy that his heart lives on in you," she said. "Can I feel it?"
He nodded and she reached out one hand and rested it on his chest, a quiet smile on her face as she felt the thump, thump, thump of her son's heart, beating its steady time, clock-like, regular.
"May I," asked Tom, stuttering a little, strangely nervous. "May I look through your photograph album?"
Mrs Morton nodded and trotted off to fetch it, brought the leather-bound object back to him. She was there, on the third page, smiling, just as she had grinned at him from the swing. A family snap; Mum, Dad, the two kids. He closed the album, thanked his donor's mother for her time and for the heart of her son, and departed.

The second memory arrived a week later, when Tom was out on his mountain bike, belting at top speed along the path that ran beside the canal behind Victoria Park, the water to his left green, murky, filled with litter; old cans of Coke, crisp packets, Kit-Kat wrappers. It was there then, the picture, as clear as if it was film footage running through his mind. A woman whom he recognised as a younger version of Mrs Morton, at the beach, kneeling in the sand, making castles which she decorated with shells and seaweed. She beckoned and extended open arms and Tom felt suddenly warm inside, glowing, as if lit by some inner sun. The memory wasn't frightening or disturbing in any way, but soft, soothing, like a cuddly toy or some other kind of pacifier. All the same, it was a little *odd* and, when he arrived home, hot, sweating, Tom (perhaps unwisely) raised the issue of the unbidden memories with Kathleen.
"I know it sounds crazy," he said. "But I think this new heart is affecting me in strange ways."
"Well, you certainly seem to have a remarkable amount of energy," his wife replied. "You're bouncing all over the place like Tigger. Truth be told, it's getting on my nerves a little. You used to be so *subdued.*"
Subdued? Bloody miserable was what he'd been, smoking forty

a day, with a heart condition and terrible circulation. Stuck in his rut of a life. Post-op he'd quit the fags effortlessly, no cravings, no crankiness, no panic attacks - all of which had stricken him on the several occasions he'd tried to stop smoking before the new heart had been put in. He didn't speak his thoughts aloud, of course, instead he said, "Well, there's that, the energy. And also the poetry. But now there's another thing, memories that don't belong to me, drifting before my mind's eye."

He described what he had seen; the girl on the swing, Mrs Morton in the sand. His wife eyed him skeptically.

"Oh Tom," she said, when he finished speaking. "It's called having an imagination, *fantasising*. Most people grow out of it. But then, most people manage to hold down a job until they retire, they don't quit when they're forty-two years old, just because they've undergone a heart transplant."

And she went upstairs to her study to mark a batch of her students' assignments. Tom made himself a cup of herbal tea (his copious caffeine consumption was another bad habit that had recently disappeared), then sat down at the kitchen table and wrote a poem that he stuck to the fridge with a magnet in the shape of a pineapple.

*Faith is the thing with wings*
*Fluttering at the window ledge*
*When all other hope has fled.*

Let her suck on that. She misunderstood him, that woman upstairs, viewed his new lifestyle as a cop-out, an abdication of responsibility. To Tom it felt as if his life, his *real* life had finally begun, as if everything up to the point in time had been merely rehearsal. The curtain had been raised, the blood sang in his veins, his old chrysalis had been shunted into the corner.

There was something else, something he didn't tell Kathleen. He was beginning to notice other women, to stare at them in a way that he hadn't done for many years; with hunger, with longing. He walked down Clapham High Street like a starving dog, tongue all but lolling from his mouth, eyes like two saucers in his head. It was disgusting. He was ashamed of himself. Yet he couldn't stop it from happening. The season didn't help - summer, legs and arms and backs hanging out of skimpy dresses, flesh every which way you looked and look he did. The more he looked, the more he cycled, seventy, eighty, ninety miles a day, until he was spending all day, every day, on his bike, to Brighton and back, to Oxford and Cambridge, to anywhere, coming home exhausted, to collapse on his bed, too tired to eat the meal that his wife had made, the dinner that was, more and more frequently 'in the dog' (even though they didn't have one). The memories kept on; visions of schoolyard bullying, of being held down by a gang of older boys, who pulled down his pants and laughed at his tiny penis, of kissing a girl on a common somewhere, up against a tree, of trombone lessons in a dusty room.

His marriage came to seem increasingly redundant, his wife a lame appendage. He would suffer nothing if she was amputated, lopped off. What had once seemed a necessity was now merely a nuisance. What need did he have for her anyway, that rapidly ageing woman who looked at him as if he was a stranger, whose smile had turned into a grimace, who refused, now, to sleep in their double bed, choosing instead to spend every night in the spare room? He wanted youth, love, vitality, not angry scowls and lips pressed tightly in disdain. Lying about his age, he booked himself on a Kontiki tour for eighteen to thirty-five year olds, went scooting off across Europe on a bus full of people whose average age was half his own, living off pizza and pasta. He drank copious amounts of sangria in Barcelona, staggered, hung over, glare-blinded, up the steps of Sacre Coeur, circled inside the Colosseum with an eighteen year old girl called Sandra on his arm. This, he told himself, was living. This was what it was all about. Sandra had sat down next to him on the first day of the tour, leant across him to push open the window, her ample young breasts full in his face, so round, so perfect, apples in need of plucking. He'd been unable, or hadn't wanted, to resist her many charms, had fallen hook, line and sinker like a foolish little trout that snaps at the first glittering fly that drifts into its line of sight. He was ensnared, he loved it, a happy insect in a sticky web, barely even bothering to struggle. What did it matter anyway, that he had a wife back in

Clapham, teaching geography to a bunch of unruly fifteen year olds, coming home late having spent hours in the classroom preparing the next day's lesson, dining alone, watching TV, falling asleep beneath the screen's blue glare? His wife was irrelevant. She didn't wear ra-ra skirts and boob tubes, didn't run her hands over his legs and chest and tell him how buff he was, had never photographed him naked in various compromising positions in random communal bathrooms across the continent. She was boring. What she didn't know wouldn't hurt her. He wasn't being malicious. He just wanted to have some fun. There were memories as well, on the European tour, some of them pleasant, some of them not so. Sometimes he tuned them out, as you would change the channel on the television, sometimes he watched them, smiling wistfully to himself, filled with somebody else's nostalgia.

On the last day of the tour, he took Sandra's number.
"Call me," she said, holding her right hand to her ear, index and pinkie fingers extended.
He smiled, knowing that he was onto a winner. Sandra was a sure bet.

Back in Clapham, there was a note on the kitchen table. *Gone to stay with Betty. Will be in touch about the house.* The faith poem had been ripped from the fridge door, torn in two, one piece placed either side of the note, a sinister, vaguely threatening little frame. Betty was Kath's sister, she lived in Battersea with a couple of vicious Alsatians, one of which had nearly taken his leg off the last time he'd been round there. What did his wife want - a divorce? Let her have it, he didn't care. He had Sandra.

Over the following days, alone in his house, he dialed the number that Sandra had given him with increasing desperation. The line rang and rang, no-one ever answered. Memories darker than those that had gone before flooded in to fill the space; an uncle pushing him to his knees, suspension from some educational institution, a girl slapping his face and shouting 'it's over!'

He cycled now, to get away from something, this thing that was after him, hot on his heels, a snapping alligator. It was like Betty's dogs, it would take a piece out of him if it could. The white lines flicking by beside him, the hot sun beating down on the back of his neck, the tar seal slick like the skin of a whale. The roads, the endless roads.

# THE GREEN-EYED SANTA

Although Mr Cookson enjoyed his life – his three children, his wife, his job at Havistock & Pritchett Chartered Accountants, the high point of every year was, for him, the week before Christmas, when he took annual leave and swapped his pin-striped trousers and neat cuffs and collars, for the bright red satin Santa suit with the lovely fake fur trim. He'd invested in the suit two decades previously, after answering a 'Santa Wanted' advertisement in the local paper. For fifty-one weeks of the year, the Santa suit hung in the back of the wardrobe, unwanted, gathering dust, stashed behind his wife's fashion strata – the mini-skirts from the sixties, the flares from the seventies, the eighties' ra-ra skirts. Come mid-December, Cookson would reach in past these clothes that had once been the height of good taste and, eyes closed, arms outstretched, he would feel, blind, for the satiny suit. That first touch was always so special, the memories it triggered, the good-times remembered - all those days when he had sat in his grotto, surrounded by fairy lights and inflatable elves, his knee a ledge for the kids to perch on. His sack full of sweeties. The cameraman ready with his Polaroid camera, finger on the button, like a man with his finger on the trigger of a gun. *Smile, smile for Santa, smile for Mummy. SNAP. That'll be £14.99 thanks, pay at the counter over there to your right.*

Cookson had never washed the Santa suit. After extracting it from the wardrobe, he would hold it to his face and inhale deeply. The suit contained all the odours of all those years; sticky sugar, sweat, mothballs, urine (more than one little tyke had got over-excited while sat upon his knee). Using a clothes brush he had bought specifically for the purpose, he would give the suit a good brushing down, and then hang it on the back of the bedroom door, in order to air it. It needed airing. It stank and he knew it. It was getting harder and harder to beat out the dust. One year there had been a spider web hanging from the left armpit. The truth was he couldn't bear to wash the suit; he was too afraid that it would fall apart for, as time passed, it grew ever more fragile, ever more threadbare. It was worn for only one week a year, but that week was a hard week; in those seven days, the suit took a right royal pummelling. He didn't dare take it to the dry-cleaners – he was frightened that they would lose it, or shrink it, or ruin it in some other terrible, unspecified way. For, in Mr Cookson's imagination, his powers, his *Santa* powers, lay not within himself, but in his suit. Without it, he was nothing. He didn't know how and he didn't know why, but the garment was charmed. When he donned his Santa outfit, he was no longer Cookson, and nor was he just another Santa, just another dumb guy in red shouting *ho, ho, ho*. Like Superman, like Spiderman, like Wonder Woman, once inside his suit, he was something else entirely, something extraordinary. Or so he had thought.

Certainly, over the years, he had been popular. The kids flocked to him as if he piped some invisible music that filled the air around him with enchantment, drawing them in. His sweets were nothing special, they were hard-boiled, bought in bulk from Woolworths, in a range of colours and flavours, yet the kids couldn't seem to get enough of him, of the sweets, of the photos. No wonder the mall kept asking him back; he'd made them a small fortune over the years. He had come to think of his 'Santa show' as something he performed not through desire, but through necessity. They needed him. Everybody knew that he was the best. Or he had been. But now there was somebody else, somebody new, working not in a shopping mall like Cookson, but out there, in broad daylight, in the middle of the 'pedestrian's only' section of the main shopping street, where he could grab the punters before they even entered the mall, *usurp* the children, steal them away.

Cookson had been hit, hit hard. This newcomer, Almond, had everything that Cookson had and more. His elves were not inflatable, but real people, little people, dressed up in elf suits. *Dwarves*, they used to be called, before the world went all politically correct. Cookson's elves could be popped, deflated. (Cookson knew this because one year a kid who went by the name of 'Griller' had sunk his gnashers into one of them, and the elf had gone down with a slow hiss, like a punctured bike tyre). Almond's elves could walk and talk and dance and sing. They were interactive. Cookson's grotto was a small dark cave, lit only by the fairy lights. Almond's base was the size of a small shop. He had three-metre-high tropical pot-plants and a water feature slightly Oriental in theme, he had real butterflies that did not fly away, but stayed, fluttering in the children's hair, he had stuffed toys that he did not sell, but rather, gave away for free, he even had a couple of trained monkeys that gibbered and jabbered and pulled at the children's clothes. There was a macaw that muttered profanities, but only when parents were out of earshot. There was a mechanical reindeer that rocked as a rocking horse would - for fifty pence you could yeehah on the fibreglass beast for seven and a half minutes, one hand clutching an antler, the other hand waving free. Almond had everything. A trailer parked up behind the rocking reindeer served chips and burgers and soft drinks and greasy hotdogs covered in deep-fried onion rings with a choice of four sauces. How on earth could Cookson compete with all of that?

He muttered under his breath about Almond's setup. *Bloody freak show. Tacky as hell. More of a lair than a grotto. Cheating, that's what it is. There should be laws governing these things. Rules. Fair's fair.* He muttered about the children. *Fickle. For years I've given them what they've wanted, boiled sweets and snapshots, a decent knee to sit on. No loyalty. That's the problem. The minute somebody bigger and brighter comes along, they're off.* But no amount of muttering could change the cold, hard facts. He'd been outmaneuvered, upstaged, in a spectacular display of one-upmanship. Last year he'd had his photo taken with fifteen kids an hour, the little brats just kept on coming, almost as if they were on some sort of conveyor belt. There'd been a three-minute limit imposed on his knee (*off, off, off*, his assistant would start shouting, if anybody tried to hog the precious lap of Santa). This year he was lucky if he was snapped with five kids per day. He'd not even had to hire an assistant – for once, he could manage the job, or lack of it, on his own. Minute after minute, hour after hour, day after day, he sat in his grotto, waiting for something to happen to Almond and his stupid elves and his ridiculous monkeys and his horrible little butterflies. He wished for a fire to break out, or for lightening to strike, or for some kind of electrical fault to bring the whole thing crashing to a screeching halt. Nothing happened. Day in, day out, Almond continued to milk it, the ringmaster of his sordid little circus, while Cookson relentlessly sulked, with every tick of the clock slumping a little further into his deep blue pit of despair.

The irony of it was, in the *real* world, the *normal,* the *everyday* world, Almond was nothing, less than nothing. Cookson knew this because the two of them worked at the same firm. Almond (first name, Zachariah, though everybody called him Zach) worked in the mailroom, sorting the mail on its way in, on its way out, picking up from, and delivering to, the various designated 'mail points' (coloured plastic trays) about the office. He was a quiet guy, softly spoken. *Wouldn't say boo to a goose* – that was what they said about Zachariah. Nobody had ever said that about Cookson, who was known for his bawdy jokes, his witty repartee, his general air of ribaldry. He'd done a stand-up routine at last year's Christmas party, pulled it off, even though he'd been exhausted after a hard day playing Santa. He'd had them rolling in the aisles.

"That guy always reminds me of David Brent," he'd heard one of the secretaries whisper, as he'd sat back down in his seat.

He'd ignored her comment. He was good at ignoring.

Some things, however, are simply too large to be pushed into the spare room at the back of the mind, and the new Santa on the block was one such phenomenon. Cookson couldn't help but think that Almond's rival grotto was a thing created out of spite. Pure malice. He wasn't doing what he did to light up children's lives, or because he enjoyed pretending to be Santa, but to show Cookson up, to make him look ridiculous. To mock and belittle him. To cut him down to size. For while Zach beavered away at his mundane 'career' (if you could call it that), sorting and weighing and stamping all those letters, Cookson's debits and credits were finally starting to add up - he was close to making partner. Havistock & Pritchett was about to become Havistock, Pritchett & Cookson, though personally, Cookson was more in favour of Cookson, Havistock & Pritchett – did it not make more sense for the names to be in alphabetical order? His suggested company name, however, had been vetoed by the firm's two existing partners. *Throwing their weight around,* Cookson had thought to himself, when he'd been forced to accept that his name would come last.

The promotion was due to take place early in the New Year; at least, that's what Havistock had told him when they'd met in October to discuss the matter. Everybody in the office knew that Cookson was soon to rise to the highest level within the firm – he'd bragged about it often enough. Word travelled. No doubt the news had pushed Almond over the edge, made him lose his sanity. Forced him into thinking that he had to compete, prove his manhood in any way that he could. *He went postal* - wasn't that what they said, when somebody lost it and took to their colleagues with an AK47 or a machete? Almond had gone postal. The butterflies were bullets in disguise.

Cookson's wife was markedly devoid of sympathy.
"It's not *his*, all that stuff he has with him. He's a Santa for hire, just like you. It's the council that have got all the gimmicks in. I read about it in the paper. They're trying to raise the town profile. They're helping us make a name for ourselves. Some towns have a giant plastic pineapple, others an over-sized fibreglass trout. Everybody needs a tourist attraction."
"But this is just one week a year!"
"Yes, but an important week, when people spend a lot of money."
"Whatever," Cookson replied, and stomped off to his study to work on his latest Ravensburger jigsaw puzzle.
He could have completed it weeks ago, had there not been so much sky.

There was more salt waiting to be poured into the wound. Almond was planning a parade, a grand parade. On Christmas Eve, he would take to the streets. Strictly speaking, both Almond and the council (who were reportedly to pay him a small fortune for his efforts) were responsible for the foul extravaganza, but Cookson knew that the parade must have been Almond's idea, his brainchild. His mind's sordid offspring. Only Almond would wish to humiliate him in such a manner.
    Cookson heard all about the pre-parade preparations from his wife. She wouldn't shut up about the damned thing. The parade was the talk of the town. An extra large float had been hired to carry that ridiculous pseudo-Santa and his elves

and monkeys and God only knew what else down the centre of the main street at midday. Why did he not just go whole hog and build a bloody ark? The parade would start down by the river and end up at the cathedral. They had been granted special permission to drive through the 'pedestrians only' area where Almond was now situated. There would be a police escort. Balloons and streamers would be tied to the edges of the float; the street would be strewn with sweets. Nine reindeer had been ordered in; not fake beasts, but real ones, shipped over from Norway. They would lead the parade, prance out front, heads held high, hooves clacking, hind quarters twitching gaily.

"Bit cruel, isn't it," Cookson remarked to his wife. "Bringing them all that way?"

"Good with juniper berries," she mused absent-mindedly. "I had that once at Zilly's."

Zilly's? Who had she been going to Zilly's with? Certainly, he'd never taken her – the restaurant's prices were far too exorbitant, a total rip-off. Cookson was a frugal man; he counted pennies for a living. Frowning, he forced his mind back to the reindeer.

"What if some of them die on the way over?" he continued. "And surely they're not used to crowds. If the journey doesn't kill them, the fright might."

"Oh, they'll be fine. They're going to dolly up the nose of one with red paint, you know. He'll be in front of the others, as is tradition. I'm looking forward to the parade actually. So are the kids. They've been speaking of nothing else all week."

Silently, steadily, Cookson bashed his head against an invisible, thoroughly solid, brick wall.

He was lying in bed on the morning of the day before Christmas Eve, when his wife called him to the telephone. Pritchett's secretary was on the other end of the line. The two partners wanted to meet with him later on that morning. Could he come into the office?

"But this is my week off," he protested. "Santa week."

"Yes we're quite aware of that," said the secretary primly. "Don't worry, the meeting won't take long. Mr Havistock and

Mr Pritchett are both here now. If you wouldn't mind just popping in for, say, ten, fifteen minutes?"

"Alright then," he grumbled. "But I hope it doesn't take up too much of my precious time."

"Oh no," came the reply. "I can assure you that it will be very quick."

She sounded like a veterinarian about to put the family pet to sleep.

They were waiting for him. They sat in the same room, at the same desk, couched in two big black leather armchairs. They were on the same side. On the other side of the desk, nearest the door, sat a small, grey plastic chair. Pritchett motioned for him to sit and he sat. He felt like a naughty schoolboy who'd been called to the headmaster's office. He had been summoned.

"Good morning, Cookson," said Pritchett, twiddling a pen between thumb and forefinger.

"Morning," said Cookson, trying to make his voice sound light, carefree.

He would be bright. He would be breezy.

"How's everything?" enquired Havistock.

"Fine. Everything's fine."

"We won't keep you long," said Pritchett. "We know you have important matters to attend to today."

The corner of his mouth turned up in a smile that bordered on a sneer.

"To cut to the chase," he continued, "we've been discussing your promotion and, contrary to what I told you earlier in the year, I'm afraid that we just can't make you partner in the New Year."

He glanced at Havistock. The two of them were fighter pilots; each backed the other up. Cookson felt himself go down in flames.

"We just don't think you're ready for it," said Havistock. "The extra responsibility can be very stressful."

What could he say? It was their company, their decision to make. What did it matter to them that he'd already told his friends, his colleagues, his wife, his children, that he was to be promoted in January? What did they care about the humiliation he'd suffer, having to tell all these people that he'd been wrong, that he'd jumped the gun, that he was to remain in his current role of Senior Accountant for another year, or five years, or decade, or until the end of his working life? The truth was simple enough to comprehend – they didn't care. He'd been beaten fair and square. He was outnumbered.

"Thank you," he said. "Thanks for letting me know."

"Merry Christmas," said Pritchett. "We'll see you in the New Year. Your old desk will be waiting for you. Say hello to your wife for me, will you?"

He didn't go to the mall. He felt he couldn't face it. His grotto stood empty. Nobody inflated the elves, nobody strung up the fairy lights. The photographer would arrive on time, wait for half an hour, realise that Santa was doing a no show, and leave. He didn't want to go to his grotto, but he didn't want to go home either. His wife would be there, in the house, pottering about in the kitchen. She would badger him. *What did Havistock and Pritchett have to say? Why aren't you at the mall? Are you looking forward to tomorrow's parade?* What he really wanted was an exit door, an escape route, a way to get from here to somewhere else, so that he wouldn't have to feel tomorrow's degradation slice through him like the sharpest of knives. He wanted to make of his index finger a magic wand, so that he might draw an invisible door in the air and then step right through it. But he could do no such thing. He was stuck in the here and now. So instead, he drove, got in behind the wheel of his car, manoeuvred his way out through the city traffic, ducking and diving, weaving in and out, until he arrived at the main road out of town. As soon as he hit the open road, he floored it, put his foot down, pedal to the metal. He had no destination. He drove just to feel the tar seal beneath his tyres, just to see the white lines flicking by; he was driving just to drive.

After an hour or so, he slowed down, shifted from full steam ahead to a meandering dawdle. He was off the main drag now, tootling along some country road which could never take him home. Fields stretched out on either side of him, fences made of wire, fences made of stone, various animals - sheep, cows, geese. Why had they not flown south already?

When he saw the beasts, he could hardly believe his eyes, could barely believe his luck. He pulled over, parked up, got out of the car and went to lean against the gate that kept them in; this gate that was all that came between them and the road. It was them alright, the reindeer, unmistakeable, all nine of them together, all in one place, as if they had been gathered there just for him, although he knew that it was Almond they had been put there for. Dasher, Dancer, Prancer, Vixen, Comet, Cupid. Donner and Blitzen née Dunder and Blixem. Thunder and lightning, to the Dutch. Oh yes, he knew all their names. And there was little Rudolph, singled out already, his nose painted a bright cherry red. He stood apart from the others, as if he fancied himself different, unique. Stuck up. Cookson had always hated the Rudolph story – the one with the red-nose teased by the other reindeer, but chosen by Santa to lead the way through the fog. Singled out for salvation. That wasn't the way the world was. Those teased in childhood ended up mercilessly inflicting themselves upon the world, like Bill Gates, or mass-murdering, like Charles Manson or Ted Bundy, or else wasting away in mental institutions, undone by the demons they had shouldered in their formative years. There *was* no Santa. Nobody could save you but yourself. He felt a special loathing now, looking at the dozy red-nosed creature as it nonchalantly grazed on the grass that sprouted beneath its feet. Rudolph would get no special treatment from him. Stepping back from the fence, he eyed the reindeer collectively, took them in as a whole, as a group. Those creatures were there for the taking. They were his prey.

Cookson returned to his car. He waited until it grew dark. He waited until no other cars passed him by. He waited. *The vulture*, he told himself, *is a patient bird.*

When he was ready, when the time was right, Cookson left his car and stood up against the fence, staring at the reindeer. There were no streetlights out here; the moon and the diamond stars provided his only illumination.

"Hello, my little friends," he whispered in the darkness.

He undid the latch, opened up the gate.

"Come on Prancer," he whispered. "Come on Vixen. Roam free. Now's your chance."

The bloody things were so stupid they didn't even try to make a bolt for it.

"Wake up," he hissed. "Wake up and run."

They weren't in the least bit interested. Some of them were lying down sleeping, others lazily grazing. One or two stared directly at him with wide, startled eyes. None of them moved. There was nothing else for it; he would have to enter their enclosure. He passed through the gate, got in behind the reindeer, and began barking like a sheepdog. The sleepers awakened, rose groggily to their feet. The eaters stopped munching. Now all of them stared at him, eighteen eyes that seemed to bore right through him.

"Move it!" he yelled, waving his arms about wildly and they scampered, finally, across the field and out through the gate.

He shooed them down the road, ran behind them for a mile or so, till he was so out of breath he couldn't continue. Would they be hit, in the morning, by moving traffic? Very well then, they would be hit by moving traffic. It wasn't his problem. None of it was his problem, not anymore.

He was not yet done. On the way back into town, he pulled in at a service station and bought two cans of spray paint – one can of white, one can of red. Rose White, Rose Red. Snow and blood. When he arrived at his house, he did not pull into the driveway but instead, parked a little way down the street, then crept into his own garage and picked up the axe that he used for chopping firewood. Prowling about in his own house like a thief. It was himself that he was stealing from.

"That you dear?" he heard his wife call, but he didn't answer, choosing instead to sneak back to his car and drive downtown to where his rival's lair lay waiting. He would take Almond down, not just because he wanted to, but because he *had* to.

'Santa's Grotto' proclaimed the sign in large red letters. As if it was the only one. With his can of red spray paint, he added an extra 'n' to the end of Santa, before the apostrophe. With his white paint, he blanked out the consonant third from the left. That was more bloody like it. The grotto had been locked up for the night but this was of no concern to Cookson. He smashed the lock with his axe, pulled open the door. What could he vandalise? What could he destroy? He lifted the axe high above his shoulders and brought it smacking down into the back of the rocking reindeer. The fibreglass beast split neatly in two, like an apple sliced in half. Cheap Taiwanese shit. A large metal spring sproinged out the back, where the rear haunch used to be. He could hear the monkeys jabbering in their cage. The butterflies flitted. Why did they not fly through the door? What was wrong with these stupid animals, the geese that stayed when they should leave, the reindeer that had wanted to remain fenced in, these lingering Lepidoptera? All these creatures that preferred the cage to freedom. Cookson couldn't understand it. He hacked through the door of the monkey's cage; they bared their teeth at him and cowered. With both hands, he reached inside and pulled them out; one of them sunk its teeth into his forearm.

"Argh! Little fucker."

He shook the monkeys off, pushed them outside, threw both cans of spray paint after them to make them run. Then he took his axe to the grotto itself, hacked at the walls and the ceiling and the floor. Chopped through electric wires. Little was left intact. *Let's see Almond prance down the main street now. All he'll have is a couple of elves and an empty float. How much of an attraction is that going to be?*

*SANTA PARADE RUINED BY HEARTLESS VANDAL*, read the main headline in the newspaper the next morning and, printed beneath in smaller type, *GROTTO DESTROYED IN ACT OF MINDLESS VIOLENCE. ANIMALS ROAM FREE.* There was a photo of the graffitied sign, and another of the empty reindeer enclosure.

"Oh my," said his wife, as she sat at the kitchen table in her pink floral nightgown, clutching a mug of tea. "Who would do such a thing?"

She cast her husband a canny sideways glance.

"By the way, what did the bosses have to say yesterday, dear?"

"Nothing," he muttered. "Nothing that matters."

He lay low. Santa would be absent again today. Santa could well be absent for quite some time.

In the New Year, Cookson returned to the office. Everything was just as it had been before; the same old routines, the same monotony. At precisely eleven am, he did as he had always done - headed for the kitchen to make a cup of tea. He was a man who lived by the clock. As he passed the mailroom, he heard a strange, strangled cry, like somebody being quietly choked. Against his better nature, he poked his head round the door. Almond was sitting on a stack of undelivered mail, crying. There was nobody else in the room.

"What's wrong?" asked Cookson.

Wasn't that what you were supposed to ask, in such circumstances? Almond didn't look up.

"The one time I got to do something good," he whimpered. "Something different. And some *arsehole* had to go and ruin it. And all those kids. Think about all those kids, deprived of their parade."

"They'll get over it," said Cookson lightly.

Almond raised his eyes.

"Oh, it's you," he said. "I thought I was speaking to somebody else."

"You'll be okay. Maybe you just weren't cut out for that Santa racket. Not everybody is, you know. It can be a pretty tough game."

"I don't want your sympathy. If you knew, you wouldn't give me any."

"Knew? Knew what?"

Some inner switch in Almond flicked from self-pity to rage, a sudden thunderstorm cracking against the darkening skies.

"Oh, you poor misguided fool. Did you never catch on? I've been fucking your wife for the last twelve months. Thanks ever so much for bringing her to last year's Christmas Party."

"What do you mean? What do you mean f-f-f-f-fucking?"

"FUCKING! What's there not to understand? In, out, in, out. Up, down, up, down. You know – intercourse of a sexual nature? Not that you'd been giving her much of it, from what she told me. Said you'd been having problems getting it up. And that you refused to take Viagra. Thought you were too much of a man for medication. Yeah, too much of a *man*."

Cookson was paralysed, frozen to the spot.

"Right then," he said eventually, when he regained the power of speech. "Back to the balance sheet, I guess."

It was certainly quite a blow. She'd been sneaking around behind his back, doing the dirty - she'd chosen a mailman over him. To add insult to injury she'd gossiped to Almond about the difficulties he'd been having, over the last couple of years, standing upright when and where it mattered. Almond surely suspected Cookson of destroying his grotto - why else the outburst? This mailman would show no mercy. He would blab to the rest of the office about Cookson's failings. The whole world would know everything about him, he would be forced to stand naked, his worse secrets exposed, all his flaws magnified in the hot, white glare of the public gaze. He couldn't even bear to confront his wife. Let her do whatever she liked.

He drove home. In through the front door, *stomp, stomp, stomp* down the corridor to the bedroom. Briefcase thrown to the floor. The game wasn't over yet. More surprises were in store. On the end of the bed lay a couple of shrunken red scraps. He recognised that fabric. The satin; the former shine. His wife was in the living room, hanging wet washing out on clothes racks to dry.
"What have you done to my Santa suit?" he screeched.
His voice sounded curiously high-pitched, as if he had just been neutered. His words seemed to bounce off the corridor walls; bat squeaks, sonar.
"It reeked, dear," came the reply, her voice as smooth as butter. "So I washed it. Most of it just dissolved into nothing. So old. Too old. Can't you just go out and buy a new one?"
"You don't understand," he said, softly, to himself. "That one was precious."
It was far too late. He felt wrecked, like a ship swept up onto the rocks. All these things that he had done because he had felt that he must.

His Santa suit reduced to a useless pile of dust.

## UBERMENSCH

Although he was not the first, he was the first great success. His was the perfect genetic mix; her grandfather's alcoholism and her mother's epilepsy had been eradicated, supplanted by the synthetically perfected genes she had chosen in the lab. The height, the athletic ability, the superior intelligence, the eyes of cornflower blue – all had been carefully selected. She had carried him inside her lovingly, eaten only organic foods, taken vitamin supplements recommended by her doctor, forgone her evening glass of white wine. She had nurtured and protected him. After all, he was the future.

She had cried at his birth; the whole thing had gone so smoothly. She had expected complications; those who had gone before had always reported problems - failure of the introduced DNA to integrate correctly with the chromosomes, or abnormalities resulting from the activation of harmful genes or the inactivation of useful ones. The other parents moaned about the difficulties surrounding intelligence, due largely to the fact that it is influenced by not one, but a number of genetic factors. But *her* child, *her* baby had been born perfect. Environment would be the big question now; at home she had toys to stimulate all areas of her son's brain, a personal trainer to see that he fulfilled his athletic capabilities, a psychotherapist to ensure that his emotions were as perfect as the rest of him. It was neither nature nor nurture alone that produced excellence, but a carefully controlled combination of the two. They wanted to give their expensive son the best possible chance at the best possible life. They could afford to.

What she wanted most was to produce another Mozart; because she had been unable to buy it, creativity was the trait she desired most for her child. Nobody knew why they had sprung up throughout history, those freaks, those Beethovens and da Vincis and Van Goghs. It seemed odd to pray for a throwback; it seemed odd to pray at all. But pray she did, though she didn't know to whom, or to what. What she asked for was a son who would, above all, be remembered. She wanted him to make a difference.

On that day, the day of his birth, her husband had given her a card with the group's creed written inside in blue ink:

*We will no longer be slaves to our genes.*

She had stared at the words, wondering why she didn't feel more liberated, more in control for, certainly, she and her husband had planted themselves firmly in the driving seat of history. Not only had they altered their son; the changes they had made would affect all future generations. They had opened the door to the reconfiguration of the human species. She felt that she had stepped across a line in time; on the 'before' side, children were as nature intended, that is, to say, flawed, on the 'after' side, the children of the wealthy would move, generation by generation, step by step, closer to perfection. Life never has been fair. The rich have always had advantages over the poor; better healthcare and housing, better transport, better nutrition. Better children were simply a natural progression. Why should the couple who can afford perfection settle for anything less? Their descendants would become the new aristocracy. They would be a breed apart.

There were limits to what they would be allowed to achieve. Cross species chimeras were illegal; nobody was allowed to manufacture a baby with a hide like an armadillo, useful though they would be as soldiers. Most people instinctively recoiled from the idea of creating a kid with the night vision of an owl and supersensitive hearing cloned from a dog, and those who fancied producing such an abomination were prevented, by law, from doing so. The UN had deemed hybrids illegal, stating that they threatened the very fabric of our being. Nobody seemed sure what it meant to be human, but common sense seemed to dictate that interspecies barriers should not be broken. There were rumours about various atrocities being produced underground, in other countries; Eastern Europe and North Korea. Probably just idle speculation.

Just last year, in 2010, human germline engineering had finally been legalised in the UK and the United States. There had been much heated debate on the issue; permanent changes to the human genome that affected future generations was thought to be a risky business - Lord only knew what we might mutate into.

The proponents of germline engineering knew exactly why humanity ruled the planet - of all the species that happened to inhabit this third rock from the sun we were the strongest, the most intelligent, the most cunningly brutal. We had conquered the weaker species, asserted our status as the dominant ape, spread like a virus across the planet's surface, made it our own. Now we were learning how to conquer ourselves. This was simply evolution on fast forward; the survival of the fittest taken to its logical and biological extreme.

There were protestors, of course, though it should be noted that dissent was not rife amongst the wealthy. Every Sunday, in the slums, people marched up and down the high street bearing placards.

"People are not products," read the signs. "Don't piss in our gene pool."

The Christians were out in force.

"Don't mess with God!"

The germliners countered the Christians by stating that if God didn't want us to better ourselves in this way, why did he give us the intellectual capacity to do so? There was another truth, one that was thought by everybody, but spoken by nobody; there was no God or, if there was, were we not now, with our ability to manufacture life, to control our own evolution, at least his equal?

They were out-dated, these protestors, believing as they did that nature knew something that man did not. They failed to realise that evolution had offered up her secrets over a decade ago, when the human genome map was completed, each word in the book of life read, and only thirty thousand of them in the end, the genes. Almost everything was understood now, documented; the human brain, the human body, every genetic clue had been traced. There was only one mystery left – artistic ability.

They had left as little as possible to chance. He was home-schooled by a succession of private tutors. They did not want him to attend any educational institutions - he would be diluted there, watered down. They wanted to keep him pure. By the age of five he had mastered differential calculus, French, Japanese and English and could run a mile in under four minutes. He could long jump a distance of ten metres and displayed emotional sensitivity and empathy far beyond his years.

Everybody said how well he mixed with adults. The problem came when other children crossed his path. They instinctively distrusted his manufactured perfection, they mocked him, kicked him, pulled his hair.

"Don't they realise I mean them no harm?" he sobbed into his mother's lap, one evening. "Why do they have to make it so hard?"

She tried to reassure him that there would soon be others like him, manufactured kids, so superior to the naturals.

"But when will they arrive?" he asked. "Why are they taking so long to show up?"

He sounded like an alien speaking of the long-awaited arrival of the rest of its race.

There were no creations. There was prowess mathematical and scientific, there was the mastery of any number of languages and a remarkable athleticism, but something made, something plucked from the ether and rendered solid? No, it was beyond him. Secretly she felt that he had failed her. She had wanted an artist and got a cyborg instead. He showed no great love of music - by twenty he had composed not even a single symphony, when she had expected several masterpieces by such an age. What was wrong with the kid? Didn't he know how much he was worth? She had bought him a piano and a drum kit and a guitar and canvasses and oils and a computer upon which to write. Nothing. Maybe he was not the perfect creature they had, at first, imagined – maybe he was just another fuck-up instead. Perhaps his birth signified not some glorious dawning, but just another grotty grey day. She knew such thoughts were uncharitable; after all, he was doing his best.

On his twenty-first birthday, they presented him with the traditional key to the door, which, they told him, was the key to *their* door. It was time for him to leave home, to find his way in the world. Having completed three degrees by seventeen, he was eminently employable. He'd used the washing machine a couple of times. She'd shown him how to boil an egg. They helped him find an apartment downtown, helped him pack up his belongings, make his exit.

What she noticed most, after his departure, was that his absence barely seemed to affect their lives. It was almost as if he had never really existed, or, if he had, it was more as a 'thing' than a person. She missed him in the same way you would miss the kitchen blender, if you had misplaced it. She found it hard to pinpoint his personality traits. He was so emotionally perfect - he expressed his anger calmly, rationally, he did not kick or yell or bite; he said 'goodnight, I love you' to his parents every night; he did not hate. His behaviour gave nothing away.

"Why can't I just be ordinary?" he had asked her once.

And it had struck her then that what she had created was not something extraordinary, as she had desired, but a paragon of ordinariness, ordinariness exaggerated to the point where it became almost parodic. He was exactly like other people, only more so. Super-ordinary.

He didn't phone home that first week, nor did they hear from him during any of the weeks that followed. They hoped he was doing okay, forging his way in the world; Lord knew they'd given him every possible advantage in life.

The call came from the police just three weeks after they'd first sent him packing. He'd forgotten to lock his door at night, and when the occupant of another apartment in the same block hadn't shut the front door properly, his fate had been sealed. He'd left himself wide open, said the cops, wide open. The marauders had come in off the street, two or three or six of them, smashed in his TV and all his windows, taken his wallet, then bashed him about the head and left him for dead.

The cops knew who he was; news of her progeny had spread despite her attempts to protect him.

"How could a genius be so stupid?" a fat doughnut chewer of a policeman asked rhetorically, as he drove them to the morgue to identify the body.

They went to his apartment. The place was filthy, sordid. Old, greasy pizza boxes, empty cans of Coke and mouldy cups of coffee lay scattered about. It was clear that they'd taught him everything except how to take care of himself. Holding tightly to her husband's arm, she moved from room to room, looking for evidence of employment, or social activity, or contact with any human at all. There was nothing, just the squalor and a slight stink that was not unlike that which came from the slums on those awful days when the wind blew towards, and not away, from their apartment. Unwashed T-shirts, a dishcloth with some sort of cress sprouting out of it, an interesting looking fungus in one corner of the bathroom.

In the hallway, an old note pad, a rough etching of a butterfly.

# THE ETERNAL DISAPPOINTMENT OF THE MUCH
# ANTICIPATED EVENT

For months Stacey Howard had lived in anticipation of the event; the gigantic burning sphere three times the size of the sun and ten times as bright, with a tail that stretched the length of the sky, blazing its way across the heavens. Halley's Comet; her mother had bought her magazines, she'd borrowed books from the library, she'd watched programs on TV. Her mind was full of facts; she knew that Mark Twain had been born, and had died, in years in which the comet appeared – in his own words 'two unaccountable freaks' pre-ordained to enter and exit this world together. She knew that some people had thought that the comet was a harbinger of the apocalypse. She knew that it had, in the past, been a small thing. This time it would be big. The comet would put things in perspective; it would wash away pain and hurt. It would light up the sky, it would make people reassess their lives and help them to find new meaning. The comet was a sort of saviour; a mark in time. It would diminish all other marks. It would be the blackest line; in comparison, everything else would fade to grey.

She bought the binoculars herself. She saved for weeks, squirreling away pocket money, until she finally had sufficient funds to purchase the damned things. When she held them up to her eyes she saw a world enlarged. What had been far away was now close. She focused her magnified gaze on ordinary household objects; the cat, Tinker, as he washed himself, the dying pot plant that sat on the coffee table in the lounge, the static of the TV screen. If only her vision could stay that way forever, everything larger than life, an eternal distortion of perspective. Everything would be easier. Everything would be full.

There had been, of late, an emptiness in the house. Overnight, her father had vanished. She woke up one morning and he was gone. Typically, when she awoke, he was in the bathroom, singing to himself as he showered, but on this particular morning, the bathroom was silent. There was no song. She washed her face at the bathroom sink, wiped the sleep from her eyes, and proceeded downstairs to the kitchen where she found her mother sitting at the table with its red and white chequered cloth, crying over a hard-boiled egg and a cup of coffee. She didn't look up when Stacey entered, but kept her head down, as if trying to pretend that she didn't exist or was invisible. Stacey knew better than to ask the question that was on her lips – *Where's Dad?* Instead, she poured herself a glass of juice and sat down opposite her mother. The silence spoke volumes. The silence was larger than sound. Perhaps it wasn't so bad after all. Perhaps he'd just popped out for a bit, to fetch a newspaper or some flowers for his wife, or he'd got up early and gone to work before anybody else was awake. Perhaps her mother was crying about something else. But he wasn't there when she got home from school, and he wasn't there the next morning or the next evening either and soon enough Stacey was forced to face the facts, icy cold and rock hard though they were. He wouldn't be there at all, any more. He wouldn't be there ever. Like the Cheshire Cat he had disappeared; unlike that cat he left no smile behind - just a note that she found scrunched up in one corner of her mother's room, when she was in there looking for a lipstick to borrow (she was just beginning to experiment with make-up).

> *Couldn't do it anymore.*
> *Felt like a fraud.*

She'd overheard her mother on the phone, though Stacey was unsure whom it was that her Mum was talking to.
*He's gone off with his secretary. Christ, did he have to turn into such a cliché? If he was going to abandon us, he could've at least chosen a unique way to go – run off with a lap dancer or something. It's humiliating. Everybody giving me pitying looks and asking if I'm okay. And no, I haven't heard from him since he left. Still gotta put a brave face on it – there's Stacey to think of.*
Her mother didn't know she was being overheard; Stacey was sitting on the stairs, with her knees pulled up to her chest and her jersey stretched over her knees. A brave face. It was true – since the egg-sobbing incident there had been no more tears in the kitchen, just the same smile that bordered on a grimace, the same

perky words, the same relentless hearty good cheer, the unfunny jokes that Stacey felt compelled to laugh at. It wasn't her mother's real face of course; it was a comic mask that covered the tragic one. All of this Halley's comet would make better. All of this the comet would fix.

Three weeks after her father had made good his escape, the wild animals commenced their relentless march through the living room. Nobody but Stacey's mother could see them, but as she herself pointed out, that didn't mean they weren't really there. The boars came first, shuffling by in pairs, as if they were on their way to the arc. As if a flood was on its way. They were watching *Eastenders* when the first of them arrived and, as the final dramatic drum roll that signified the program's finale rattled out, Stacey's Mum pointed at nothingness and said "Pigs! Wild pigs! Six of the buggers!" then rose to her feet and pottered off into the kitchen, wondering aloud if she'd left out something that might attract such unusual guests. In the days that followed, other creatures appeared. Camels, tigers, bears – small black bears and larger, fiercer, grizzlies with dark greedy eyes and glistening white fangs. Ferocious things that could do untold damage with a single swipe. Nobody could work it out; Stacey's Mum couldn't understand what it was that was attracting the animals, or where they had come from, or where they were going, and Stacey couldn't understand why her mother was seeing things that nobody else could see.

"Maybe you just need a rest Mum," Stacey said, but her mother shook her head.

Stopping would make it worse, she said. Like a bicycle, forward motion was all that kept her upright. She worked as a lone parent advisor at Reed, helping solo Mums and Dads to get back to work. She liked to help. It made her feel useful, made her feel that her life wasn't a complete and utter waste of time and that she herself wasn't a complete and utter waste of space. But every night she cried, useless, endless tears that served no purpose. Tears that took her nowhere. She didn't sob in front of her daughter; she went to her room to do it. Stacey heard her through the wall – the wailing wall, as she'd come to think of it. And still the beasts from the other place, marching through the living room, some of them (said Stacey's mother) performing little dance steps, waltzes and foxtrots and whatnot. As if they were hoping to keep an audience entertained.

There was no-one to discuss these problems with. Brothers or sisters would have made it better. Siblings would have made it okay – they could've laughed at their mother behind her back, poked fun, lain in opposite beds at night and whispered reassuring words to each other. Reached out, maybe, and held hands, depending on how great the distance between the two beds was. Instead of somebody to hold hands with, there was the comet. It was inescapable, like fate. It was evidence that something or somebody higher was in control. It was proof that all was unfolding according to some plan, and part of that plan quite obviously included the animals that her mother was now seeing and the bottomless grief that she was suffering, so viewed that way, pictured in that light, there was nothing to worry about. At school, the previous term, they'd studied Troilus and Cressida.

*The heavens themselves, the planets, and this centre*
*Observe degree, priority and place,*
*Insisture, course, proportion, season, form*
*Office and custom, all in line of order*

The comet fitted right in with all of that. It was part of the natural order of things. Who in their right mind would argue with events that were divinely decreed?

And it all might have continued in this fashion; the animals, the sobbing, the stiff upper lip that Stacey kept, along with her resignation, if it had not been for the phone call from her father that came six weeks after his departure and that threatened to shatter, like a brick hurled through a windowpane, the routine that her life had fallen into. It was Stacey who answered the phone. Her father's voice sounded forced, strangled.

"I was hoping to take you out this Sunday," he said. "I thought we could go to the lake."

The lake had been their special place. It was more of a pond, really, located *bang smack* in the centre of their local common, but Stacey liked to think of it as a lake, as to do so made her feel closer to nature, connected to the earth, more than just an alienated little unit plodding her way through an indifferent world. In the winter the lake froze over and you could hire skates from a man and strap them to your feet and go spinning out across the slippery, treacherous surface. In the summer there was abundant birdlife – ducks, geese, the odd swan. It was winter now; everything would be frozen. Everything would be cold white ice. She considered turning him down, to teach him a lesson for abandoning her and her mother, but how could she say no to her own father? He was her Dad, the only one she had.

"Sure," she said. "The lake sounds cool."

"Don't tell your mother. She might start hounding me for, you know, stuff. She might start asking me to return."

"To be honest, Dad, I think she's beyond caring. I don't think she's terribly well."

"What do you mean *not well*?"

"I'll tell you all about it on Sunday."

"Meet me at the lake at about nine. Then we can spend most of the day together. Maybe go to the zoo after, if you fancy."

Animals, more animals.

"K see ya then."

She put down the phone without waiting for him to say goodbye.

There had been another lake also, one in the process of being made – it would become a dam that would supply the power station the government was planning. She'd stayed nearby as a kid. They'd cleared out an entire town to make way for it; moved all the inhabitants elsewhere. They were planning to drown the town. She and her parents had stayed in a hotel with a sign outside that read 'Soon to be on the banks of beautiful Lake Milton'. Trees were planted on either side of the sign. The hotel's owner seemed to feel that her secured location was something of a coup – she'd got the land cheap, nobody else had the foresight to realise that it would be worth a fortune one day. But the project never went ahead. Something happened – bad planning, financial or otherwise and so the woman had been left there, with a piece of what should have been prime real estate but which turned out to be a slice of land nobody else wanted or would ever want. One more loser in life's vicious lottery. It was an image that Stacey had been unable to forget, it had stuck in her mind as if burnt there with a branding iron; the woman waiting and waiting for the water to rise. The water never rising.

Sunday arrived. It was the day that the comet was scheduled to appear. *Scheduled* – it *was* the right word; the comet had been slotted into the calendar of heavenly events, and now, like a girl pulling back the window of an advent calendar she would bear witness to it, in all its fabulous greatness. It would be present during the day, but only visible by night. On the morning that it was due, she awoke feeling like she'd felt as a kid, on Christmas Day. Snow had fallen overnight. When she pulled back the curtains she saw a thick blanket of it, broken by the footprints of animals. Foxes, probably. Crows. Her mother was still in bed; that was becoming a habit, an unsavoury one, wallowing under the duvet for most of the morning when the weekend rolled around, as if she had nothing to get out of bed for. Which maybe she thought she hadn't.

Stacey made herself a cup of coffee and poured it, still steaming, into a plastic cup so she could take it with her, then dressed in her warmest woollen trousers, a jersey, a long overcoat, a hat and mittens, a stripy scarf that had been a present from her Dad for her last birthday (a way of pleasing him, of showing him that she still wanted to maintain some connection). The streets were almost completely deserted; there was nobody around. It was too early for most people. The steam from the coffee mingled with the steam coming out of her mouth. She shuffled her feet as she walked, so that when she turned to look back over her shoulder it seemed that the thing that had made its way down this pavement was more like something robotic than something human. The gates to the park were locked; she found a place where the spikes had fallen from the top of the fence, sculled the remainder of her coffee, which scalded her oesophagus as it went down, and then climbed over, catching her coat as she leapt down to the other side. Pulling herself free, she continued on her way, heading for the centre of the park, for the place where she would sit and wait.

There was a bench beside the lake; it was covered in leaves and snow. She scraped away the snow with a mittened fist and plonked herself down. It was five to ten. She was right on time; the old boy would be here soon, and then they would be able to discuss things – his departure, her mother's crumbling mental state, school. Then it was ten o'clock, and then ten past. The hands of her wristwatch continued their relentless march. She tried not to look; it seemed so cruel, the way that time just kept on, the way the wheels, the cogs, kept turning, even when you wanted them to stop. By half past ten she'd resigned herself to the fact that her father would not be appearing, that he'd done a no show, set her up just to knock her down, done it on purpose, to give himself some weird kind of kick, to gain some control over her, to play her like a piano maestro sat at the keyboard of her emotions. She would not give him the power, she would take it back. She wouldn't let him near her – she would build a wall, she would invent a persona, an interface and that would be as close as he ever got. Next time he called she would hang up. All the same, despite the feigned indifference, the internal shrug that nobody was witnessing, she felt the letdown as something almost physical – a slump, a weight falling on her slender shoulders. She walked around the lake a couple of times and then headed back home.

Her mother was in the living room watching *Songs of Praise*. The songs sounded strange as if they were coming up from underwater, as if the people singing them were mer-people - part-fish. A choir with scales and tails.

"Christ, Stace," said her mother, looking over. "Why the long face? What's happened?"

"Nothing."

"You know what night it is tonight, don't you? Comet night. So, cheer up. Isn't this what you've been looking forward to for so long?"

"Yes and no."

"What do you mean love? What do you mean yes and no?"

"I dunno, it just doesn't seem…"

"Seem what?"

"Worthwhile anymore."

What could you say to that? What could you say to a daughter who'd suddenly decided that the thing she'd most anticipated was no longer worth witnessing? Nothing. And nothing was what her mother said, just settled back down on the sofa, her eyes once more on the TV, as riveted as if *Songs of Praise* was a celestial, rather than a terrestrial, broadcast.

Later on that day her father called.

"Hello love, shame we missed each other this morning."

She tried to hang up, but couldn't quite bring herself to put down the receiver. He had his excuse to hand.

"I couldn't get into the park," he said. "The gates were locked. I tried to call your mobile but it just rang and rang. Didn't you take it with you?"

"No, I forgot it."

"So let's meet next Sunday then."

"No," she said. "No I don't think so Dad, sorry. I'm meeting someone."

"Meeting someone? Who?"

"Just a friend. No-one you know Dad – a new friend from school. We've already agreed to do something together on that day."

"Oh right. The week after then?"

"No sorry. Busy then too."

"Stace! Stop being so unreasonable."

"I'm not being unreasonable! It's just, y'know…I waited there for you today and you didn't show up."

"I told you, the gates were locked. You know that yourself."

"Whatever. I'll see ya round."

He was telling the truth. Her mobile lay on the bed. She had several missed calls.

*Oh well,* she thought, *fuck it. If he'd wanted to see me that badly he would've climbed the fence like I did. It was just an excuse, saying that the gates were locked. If I agree again to meet up with him, he's only going to let me down. I can't be his puppet. I won't let him pull the strings.*

Night fell. Her mother was still on the sofa; she'd been there all day, she hadn't even moved to fix herself a cup of tea, or a bowl of soup for her lunch, or any of the other basic, fundamental things that she typically did on a Sunday such as mop the kitchen floor or clean the bathroom. No doubt she was too engrossed with the creatures that she was seeing; as if the illusions that she conjured were more real to her than this world. Stacey walked out into the back garden and held the binoculars up to her eyes. It was better outside; outside was always preferable to in. It was a bright, clear night; crystalline. The stars hung in the sky like cold white diamonds. There it was, high in the heavens. Not even the size of a marble; more like the head of a pin, but too small, even, for angels to dance on. A feeble thing, pale, barely glowing. Where was its blazing tail? It was barely on fire. It was the very definition of disappointment. It looked nothing like the pictures in the books, nothing like the object that she had imagined. It was as if the comet, the *actual* comet, had decided to pull a sickie and sent along its understudy to take its place. Even the stars, the everyday stars, upstaged it.

Back inside the house, she hung up her binoculars; looped their thin leather strap over the hat rack in the hall.
"They've stopped," said her mother. "They just suddenly ceased to arrive."
"Oh dear, that's a shame."
She was tired of it now, the madness that didn't quite ring true, but struck instead, a hollow chord. She traipsed up the stairs to her room. This is what there was; this was all there was. Objects that should appear but don't; things that are smaller, fainter, paler, feebler than you imagine them to be; tasks that are begun but never finished. Events that are never on time.

# SPACE INVADERS

He left because he thought that aliens were planning to invade. For weeks he'd sat out on the front porch, scanning the skies in search of a mother ship, the shotgun that he used to shoot ducks with resting in his lap. Mostly he was silent, but from time to time he would shake his fist and yell, "Come on ya bastards, I'm ready for ya. Bring it on. Bring it bloody *on.*" My sister Katrina and I had tried to convince him to calm down and be sensible and come inside, but he wasn't having any of it. He even slept out there, dozing in his chair, his head falling down to rest on his chest, just little cat naps, nothing major. He often stayed awake right through the night; he said that he didn't want them to catch him sleeping. *That,* he said, would be the end of the world.

"Could be I'm the only thing that comes between them and the destruction of humanity," he'd say. "Without me the rest of you could be doomed, *doomed.*"

"Christ, who does he think he is?" I said to Katrina. "The saviour of mankind. *Please.* Spare it."

"Just leave him," Mum said, when we gathered around Dad's chair, begging and pleading with him to quit acting like a crazy man and come inside and join the rest of us. "Leave him be."

She took him plates of food – corned beef and spuds, spaghetti bolognaise, roast beef with horseradish sauce. He would pick half-heartedly at the meal, and then put the plate down on the porch, lean back in his chair and yell, "Tea, Moira. More tea." He took it black, strong, three teabags in every cup, no sugar, drank it in vast quantities, ten or more cups a day, gulping the hot liquid back. It kept him upright and alert. It kept him going.

He claimed to have picked up messages regarding the invasion on one of the many radios he collected, that were kept in the garden shed. Pre-invasion fever he'd been an accountant - he worked for a local firm, Johnson & Regus. A bean counter. He considered the work beneath him; he'd assumed that life held greater things in store. He was crippled by the gap between what he'd wanted to achieve and what he wound up attaining. He hadn't intended to end up in the suburbs, locked in his white picket fence life, a salary slave. He'd hoped to become a great inventor, summoning up creations such as never before known to humankind. The da Vinci of his generation. But instead of dreaming up the modern day equivalent of a helicopter prototype, such as (for instance) a spaceship that could glide to distant planets, he tallied up debits and credits, his days lost in a haze of Excel spreadsheets and meaningless graphs. He had the notion that somewhere, ages back, he'd taken a wrong turn, gone left when he should've gone right, pulled into a parking bay when he should've kept driving. Simultaneously, contradictorily, he seemed to think that it was not *him* who had made bad decisions, but *fate* who had dealt him a cruel blow, refused to take care of him, let him down in indescribable ways. Attempting to drown the disappointments of his life, he threw himself into his hobbies. His evenings had settled into a predictable routine. He would sit at the dinner table, unspeaking, mechanically eating his food, like a wind-up toy. Before the rest of us were even half-finished he'd push back his chair and head out to the shed, leaving his plate for his wife to clear away. He'd lurk out there in the shed for hours, wiring and re-wiring, twiddling with dials, seeing what he could pick up on short wave, before returning inside and falling asleep beside his wife.

On the afternoon that he was made redundant he came home and, without even breaking the news to the rest of us about his loss of job, he'd gone straight out to the shed. That was when the message had arrived, crackling, like thunder rolling in across the ocean. He didn't tell us exactly what was said, but when he came back into the house he was convinced that an invasion was imminent. He was distracted, wide-eyed, twitchy, like a man possessed. Restless, he paced the house, unable to sit still for more than a second. Ants in his pants.

"Harold," said my mother. "Harold, what is it?"

"Nothing," he said. "Nothing."

"Well, it must be something."

"Alright, alright, I've been made redundant."

"Oh love. Oh *love*. Listen, never mind. You'll find another job. And weren't you starting to get tired of that one anyway? You pulled an awful lot of sickies over the last five years. You seemed to be home more often than not."

"Yea whatever."

He continued pacing, walking the length of the lounge and back, ceaseless, relentless, like a caged jungle animal.

"Is that all? Is there something else you're not telling me?"

He shot her a fierce, dark look.

"They're *coming*," he said. "They're on their way."

His eyes were wide, ferocious, possessed. He turned on his heels and stomped back out to the shed.

I followed him, but only so far. I stood outside, beneath the Milky Way with its wild, wheeling stars, the moon full and bright overhead. For a long time I lingered there in the darkness, looking in through the lit window of the shed as, inside, my father hunched over one of his renovated radios, his head pressed up to the speaker, waiting for further messages to come through. *God help us*, I thought. *What will become of us now that the old boy's gone round the twist?*

It had been a gradual thing. It was not out of the blue. There had been signs.

As a child, my father had been struck by lightning. He'd been following his own Dad round the golf course acting as caddy when it'd happened, electricity falling from the sky, a jagged, spiteful finger, avoiding all the other golfers and striking him in the head. Why him? What'd he had that made him so special, that'd singled him out as a target? Why had he been chosen and the others ignored? It hadn't hurt; it was over so quickly that he hadn't really known too much about it. He woke up in hospital with second degree burns, three of his four limbs in bandages. His eyebrows and eyelashes had gone, along with half of the hair on his head.

*What am I doing here?* he asked, and later *What's my name? Can anyone remember my name?*

*Harold*, a nurse told him softly. *Your name's Harold.*

But the name itself didn't mean anything; it was attached to an empty vessel. It didn't belong to him, nothing did, nothing was his anymore. He'd been wiped out, obliterated. He searched his mind for memories, but found none. He was a blank slate; tabula rasa. The doctor said he was lucky to be alive and that he would need careful nurturing if he was ever to return to full health. It was his mother, Sylvie, who tended to him, helped him understand who he'd once been, who he was. She showed him photographs, as if to jog him back to himself. *Here you are fishing, standing next to me on the end of a wharf. Here you are playing cricket for the school team. Here you are receiving your prize for coming first in mathematics.* Piece by piece, he remembered himself. Piece by piece, he put himself together, a patchwork made of memories, stitched together with flimsy black thread. He was a boy that could come apart at any time. He was something for Sylvie to molly-coddle. He spend the rest of his childhood cosy inside the cocoon she spun around him, often home from school, whether genuinely sick or not (a pattern that continued into his working life), envisaging his weird little visions, dreaming of the day when his inventions would conquer the world. Dreaming of all the things that would never come to pass.

By the time that Katrina and I were born, Sylvie was living with us. Her husband had died ten years earlier of lung cancer. She'd tried living alone, but she hated it, especially at night, when the ghosts came flooding in with their incriminating voices, their accusations and laments. Dad built a granny flat for her under the house and she moved in, led a self-sufficient life, did her own cooking and cleaning, had her own little patch of garden that she tended. She came upstairs a lot, fussing over our father, fussing over us. She had to have something to mother. She was big on embroidery. She would bring her latest work upstairs and sit on the sofa, needle pricking in and out of the fabric, bright colours weaving a design. I remember her, in those weeks before Dad disappeared, the porch weeks, stitching a circle in a luminescent shade of green, humming to herself the same three notes over and over, like something out of *Close Encounters of the Third Kind.* Like someone who knew something that we didn't.

It wasn't Dad who had told me about the lightning incident, it was Mum. Dad could act weird sometimes, moody and silent one minute, prone to violent outbursts the next, as if he was a lightning storm himself. As if the lightning had acted as a kind of reverse ECT – rather then balancing out his moods, it had unbalanced him. One second he would be catatonic, lying in his bed, refusing to get up and go to work, the next he would be bouncing round the house singing his heart out.

The doctor had told him to take up a second hobby to help him to relax, to distract his mind. *The radios are not enough*, the doctor said. *You need something more.* He'd chosen painting. He set up his easel in the spare room, stating, *if it's good enough for Churchill, it's good enough for me.* Sometimes Katrina and I could hear him in there late at night, throwing paint around, Pollock-style, muttering to himself. He often missed the canvas and hit the walls – they were coated in splattered colour, great, vivid dollops of it. Mum tried to convince him to put on an exhibition, suggesting that it might help boost his sense of self-worth, but he'd turned up his nose at the idea. *What do you think I am? A battery hen? Valued only for what I produce?* He clucked and flapped his arms about a bit, then went back to the spare room and cranked up the Mozart he liked to listen to while he worked. Mum felt the need to provide Katrina and me with some sort of explanation for his unpredictable behaviour. *I want you to know that your father's lived through rather a lot in his time. Things that could scar a person. Catastrophes. Acts of God. He was once struck by lightning.* She launched into the story of Dad and the golf course and how he'd once forgotten completely who he was. I didn't really understand her when she started up with that kind of talk; I thought she was just making excuses for him. *Can't he just be fixed?* I asked her one day, as she stood at the kitchen sink, peeling veges for our dinner. She stopped what she was doing, put down the peeler, spun to face me. *Your father, dear girl, is one of life's Great Unfixables. It's best you get that straight in your head.* It was as clear as a pane of newly cleaned glass – Dad was something for us to tip-toe around. Somebody to handle with kid gloves.

Our hall cupboard was full of supplies that he'd bought for when *they* showed up; canned fruit, canned veges, SPAM, candles, torches, batteries, fishing gear, the works. The items that had once resided in there, the towels, the linen, the washcloths, had been shunted onto the floor to make room for what he termed 'necessities.' When he left he took some of those necessities with him, including the fishing gear. I know this because when I woke up on that morning, the morning of his departure, the door of the hall cupboard stood open and you could see that a lot of stuff was missing. He'd taken other things as well; painkillers from the medicine cabinet, his walking stick, his shotgun, three of our best knives from the kitchen.

"Dad?" I yelled. "Dad?"

We searched the entire house but he was nowhere.

"Oh Christ," said Mum. "Oh Christ. I knew something like this was going to happen."

*If you knew it was going to happen*, I thought, *why the hell didn't you do something to prevent it*, but I didn't say anything aloud. Instead, I put one arm around her shoulders and told her that everything was going to be okay, even though I didn't really believe that it was. It wasn't until later on that evening that we found the note, penned in bright red ink, impaled on toothpicks that were stuck into a bit of steak he'd put in the fridge to defrost.

*I can't fend them off single-handedly*, it said. *The time grows nigh. Save yourselves.*

So weird. Why steak? But I'd given up, by then, on trying to understand my father's mind, his thought patterns that looped and spiralled like an out of control fighter plane, his curious little habits. His strange ways.

He'd always been unusual, but since his redundancy his behaviour had become increasingly bizarre. *There's no such thing as normal*, they say, but sitting out on the front porch for seven weeks waiting for aliens to land, then buggering off and leaving your family with nothing more by way of farewell than a note impaled to a piece of steak in the freezer would probably qualify, in most people's book, as *ab*normal. After the redundancy it's like it wasn't even really him there anymore, as if somebody else had taken up residence in his body. One of those aliens, maybe, that he'd spent so much time raving on about. Maybe it'd all been a ruse, sitting out there, waiting for them to land, all cunningly designed to throw us off his path, to keep us distracted, while his fellow invaders from outer space took up residence inside our actors, our politicians, our novelists. Took over our businessmen and women, our shopkeepers and housewives and librarians. Took over planet earth.

Nobody knew for certain where he'd gone, but I had an inkling. Years ago, my parents had invested in a second property, a small, dilapidated shack in the back of beyond, unreachable by road. The track that led down to the shack had not been made but rather, had been worn, created by decades of trampling feet. We hadn't been out there in years, so no doubt the track would've grown over, tangled creepers, interweaving vines creating a thicket, and if that's where he'd gone, then he would've been forced to hack his way through, slicing aside foliage with one of our knives. God knows what kind of state the shack would be in when he got there - windows cracked and coated in thick dust, spider webs dangling from every corner, a few old teabags in the cupboard, some instant coffee. Still, it would be a roof over his head, he could hunker down there for ages, eeking out the supplies he'd brought with him, living, in part, off the land - fishing, digging up edible roots, tearing berries from the trees. Shooting pigeons with his shotgun, roasting them over an open fire. The simple life, free from complexities. An escape – cowardly in one way, brave in another.

Katrina and I shared a room. On the night of his big exit we were lying in our separate beds, quiet in the darkness, till Katrina spoke up and said, "Do you think he's ever coming back?"

She didn't need to say who 'he' was.

"I doubt it," I said. "I reckon he's gone for good. If we want him to return, we're gonna have to go find him. Drag him back. Then again, what good is it *forcing* someone to stick around if they don't want to? Even if it is your own father."

"He's just confused at the moment. Lost. Maybe he wants to be alone for a bit. He'll come back when he's good and ready."

"No," I said. "No. He won't be coming back. Not unless we go find him."

"I ain't going nowhere. If he wants to go, let him go."

So I knew that it would be down to me. It was no great surprise. Katrina and I were twins, but we were far from identical. As kids we'd been similar, alike, two peas nestled in the same pod. Post-puberty we'd grown apart, separating from each other like the two halves of a drawbridge as it's raised. Our differences had become greater than our commonalities. In many ways she'd become my nemesis. She was as frivolous as I was serious. She was blonde, perky, cute. Everything about me was dark; my hair, my eyes, my mind. She bubbled and she bounced. Just looking at her made me feel tired. Around the same time as Dad'd been made redundant I'd been stricken by a crippling sense of apathy and inertia as if the melancholy that was supposed to hit those who suddenly lose their jobs had bypassed my father and landed *splat* on me. I slogged through my days feeling leaden, weighted; each morning it grew harder to rise. It had become difficult to concentrate on my schoolwork; words would lose their meaning before my very eyes, fail to signify. I felt buried, a bird with clipped wings. I spent inordinate amounts of time at the local video arcade playing Defender, fending off the little buggers before they landed, *pow, pow, pow*. Katrina, meanwhile, was flying. She was into extra-curricular activities in a big way; hockey, basketball, ballet, drama. She belonged to the school debating, chess and backgammon teams. She was active in the community. She went to church twice a week, did Meals on Wheels at the weekends, delivering hot dinners to elderly folks who couldn't always cook for themselves.

"You'll run yourself ragged," Mum would say, but Katrina didn't listen and, to her credit, she seemed to handle it all with ease, she never looked weary or drained.

Uberwench. But for all my melancholia, I knew that it was me that had the stronger backbone, the superior will, the greater determination. Katrina was willing to just let Dad go, waft off elsewhere, like a kite whose flier has let go of its string. But me, I couldn't give up just like that. I had to keep hanging on – it was in my nature. I didn't know how to let go.

I didn't tell anyone where I was going in person; instead, I did as my father had done and left a note, not impaled to a bit of steak, but on the kitchen table beneath a half full coffee cup.

"Gone to find Dad and bring him back," I wrote.

Short and sweet. I dressed in my warmest tracksuit, put on my hiking boots, threw a raincoat and a thermos full of tea and some nuts and raisins in a backpack. It was early in the morning when I was leaving; the sun was just beginning to rise, coming up on the far horizon, weak rays of light, diluted. I walked as far as the main road, out through the quiet suburban streets, the curtains still drawn in the windows of the houses, everybody still sleeping. I stuck out my thumb. Two cars passed me without stopping, and then a third, a large brown Holden, pulled over. A guy with a bushy black beard wearing aviator shades leaned over and pushed open the passenger door.

"Hey kid, where ya off to?"

"Totara," I replied, naming the nearest township to our shack, the place where the roads faded out into nothingness.

"Totara it is. Hop on in."

"Well, I mean, only if you're going there anyway."

"I'm going there now, kid, I'm going there now."

"Cool."

I jumped in beside him, slammed shut the door. He was covered in tattoos; more ink than skin. Motorhead blared.

"You like Lemmy?" he asked, gesturing with his thumb towards the stereo.

"Yea," I said, "Yea. Lemmy's alright."

He cranked up the stereo even louder, hung one arm out the window, drumming his fingers on the car door. I stared straight ahead, mouth set in a firm, straight line, my arms folded across my chest, everything about my demeanour discouraging conversation. My driver was not to be deterred.

"Yea, going down to Clapton to see a mate who's just been let out of clink. In there for murder. He was innocent of course."

"Of course. Everybody always is."

"Na man, I mean, *really* innocent, not just bullshitting."

"Right."

He continued in this vein until Totara, harping on about the innocence of his friend. I was glad to get out of that car, glad to see the back of him, happy to see his vehicle receding into the distance, smaller and smaller, till it was nothing but a speck on the far horizon.

I walked from the main road to where the track started. You could see that somebody had been down there recently. Branches were broken, snapped twigs were strewn hither and thither. Recent rain had left the path slippery, and I made my way down tentatively, skidding from tree trunk to tree trunk, taking great care not to fall. The door of the shack stood open. He'd definitely been here, and recently. I could smell him in the air.

The shack consisted of just two rooms; the first was the bedroom, which had two bunks in it, and a couple of sleeping bags bunched up in the corner. Army gear. Standard issue. The other was the main living area, which had a kitchen at one end of it – just a sink and a couple of cupboards. No cooker, though. There was an old gas ring next to the sink. The paint was peeling from the kitchen cupboards, falling to the floor in flakes. Pulling open one cupboard, I found a box of candles, a few old teabags, a couple of tins of baked beans, a jar of instant coffee, some matches. In a drawer beneath the cupboard, various utensils; a fork, a spoon, a couple of rusting knives. I lit a candle and placed it on a saucer in the middle of the table, then used the same match to get the gas ring going. Wind gusted in through a crack in the wall; the flame flickered. I heated up the baked beans and ate them straight from the can.

I'd never spent a night alone in the shack before, there'd always been somebody else there, somebody else to light the candles, somebody to play bridge or Scrabble with, somebody to keep the dark night away. There seemed to be eyes out there in the darkness, eyes that watched me, eyes that bored holes in the wall, strange creatures that lurked, hybrids with the head of a deer and the body of a bull, or the head of a jackal and the body of a crow, twisted animals, Jabberwockies, fictional things. Products of an over-active imagination, but no less real for the fact that they had been summoned up, conjured out of thin air. I lay rigid on the top bunk as the wind whistled by outside, shrieking like the voices of the dead. The kind of sound that could drive you insane if you let it.

In the morning it was raining, water falling from the sky, as thick and grey as misery. I pulled on my raincoat, stepped out into the downpour. Vines tangled my hair, grabbing at me like the fingers of witches. Up ahead, a clear patch of ground where the trees had been felled
"Dad," I yelled. "Dad?"
God only knew what state he'd be in when I found him, what unnameable horrors I would find. Would he be filthy and scab-ridden, the Great Unwashed, would he be scrabbling round in the dirt looking for grubs, would he have lost his mind? I was Dorothy hunting down the Wizard of Oz; I was Marlow searching for Kurtz. I was everybody who goes searching for somebody, not knowing what they will find.
There he stood in the clearing. He wore a green papier mâché alien mask. The eyes on it were enormous, white and bulging, bug eyes. A tube hung from his mouth, held on by a thick black elastic strap that encircled his head. It looked like a piece of old vacuum cleaner hose. It made him look elephantine. He was making weird noises, like a cornered animal, breathing in and out through that tube. Snuffling.
"They got me," he said. "They got me. I'm one of them, dear, I'm one of them. Get away, get away."
*O God,* I thought, *I can't deal with this. I shouldn't have come out here on my own; I should've brought somebody else with me, Mum or Katrina, Sylvie, even. Someone to help me handle the horror of this sight.*

There was a whirring in the sky and then a great sucking sensation, like being hoovered up inside a tornado.
"We come in peace," I thought I heard somebody mutter and then there was nothing, just the vast darkness of outer space and the earth a tiny, spinning blue and green marble receding beneath the two of us as we were beamed up into the heavens.

## HALLOWEEN IN THE ANTIPODES

Adults in New Zealand in the 1980s didn't believe in Halloween. They seemed neither to understand nor to appreciate the cultural invasion that their children welcomed with such open arms. They were in denial. But Sheryl and I had faced up to the truth; the United States was cool, New Zealand was embarrassing. What did we have going for us other than sheep and rugby? Peter Jackson had not yet put us on the map; we had not yet become Middle Earth, we were still the end of it – the arse end. When I looked on my brother Kane's blow-up globe, I saw that we were right at the bottom of the world, next stop Antarctica. The Artic, of course, was at the top.

"Why can't it be the other way round?" I had asked my brother when I had first examined the globe.

"Don't be daft," he said. "If you did that then America would be in the bottom half of the world and *that* wouldn't make any sense."

He didn't mention China or Russia or Canada or Europe and how they would feel about being relegated to the lower half of the atlas; only America, by which he meant North America, the United States.

"Cops of the world," said Dad, sipping his local beer.

He had been listening from the next room. But he didn't know anything.

America seemed to have all the good stuff. Take, for instance, the national symbol – in both cases, coincidentally, a bird. The United States had the eagle, fierce, defiant, beady-eyed, soaring high through friendly skies. We had the kiwi, a flightless, nocturnal creature, cursed with an over-sized proboscis, with which it snuffled around in the dirt, looking for grubs. Surely it didn't bode well. Japan, I was told one day at school, had the rising sun; symbol of hope and of some unspecified future promise.

"Which country has the setting sun?" I asked that night at home. I was full of annoying questions.

"No country," said my father. "Go run round in the backyard." I never seemed to get enough answers.

Sheryl and I knew what to do. If we couldn't be American, we would pretend to be. We read Nancy Drew and Archie comics, watched endless reruns of *Little House on the Prairie* and made appalling stabs at the accent. We listened to Dolly Parton and Kenny Rogers. My favourite song was *The Gambler*; I knew all the words. Sheryl was in love with *Magnum P.I.* Kane, an avid reader of history books, had tried to talk to us about the Munroe Doctrine, the New Deal, the Cuban Missile Crisis, Martin Luther King, Vietnam, the Cold War, but we didn't care about all of that. We wanted the culture, not the history. *Happy Days*, not Watergate.

And then there was Halloween. This particular custom was considered to be one of our favourite country's finer points; we would appropriate it, make it ours. A week before October the thirty-first, we decided that, come that date, we would haunt the neighbourhood, taking from the locals what sweets or, rather, *candy* we could. I didn't really know what would be involved; I had vague ideas about pumpkins and ghouls. Sheryl filled me in on the finer points.

"Basically," she said, "you go round knocking on doors dressed up as something scary and making vague threats and they give you stuff. *Candy*. And what you say is 'trick or treat?' It's a question, you know. You give them the choice. "

"Cool," I said.

The idea of getting something for nothing held a lot of appeal. My father said that Halloween was Yankee garbage.

"Actually," said Kane, when he heard us talking, "Halloween is derived from the ancient Celtic festival of Samhain which took place when the year changed from light to dark, and winter began to descend. At this time, the spirits of the dead were supposedly able to enter the world. The townspeople baked food all day and, when night fell, they dressed up and tried to resemble the dead, hoping to fool the spirits into thinking that they were just like them, on their side. They would leave food on the edge of the town, praying that, if they satisfied the ghosts, they would be left in peace."

"Fascinating," said Sheryl, snapping her bubble gum at him.

But Kane wasn't finished.

"Carving pumpkins into jack-o'lanterns is another Halloween custom that originated in Ireland. A legend grew up about a man named Jack who was so stingy, so much of a miser, that he was not allowed into heaven when he died. He couldn't enter hell either because he had played jokes on the devil. So, with nowhere else to go, Jack was condemned to walk the earth with his lantern until Judgment Day. The Irish people carved scary faces out of turnips, beets or potatoes representing "Jack of the Lantern," and when they brought their customs to the United States, they carved faces on pumpkins because, in the autumn, pumpkins were plentiful."

"Right little encyclopaedia, your brother. Go on then, smart arse, what sort of jokes did he play on the devil?"

Kane shrugged.

"I dunno," he said. "It's just a myth."

"Don't worry about him," I said. "Come on, let's go outside."

I didn't want to be like my brother; all brains and no friends. I led Sheryl out to the garden, where we sat on a wooden bench and discussed our planned activity.

"What shall I dress up as?" I asked, looking to her, as usual, for guidance.

Sheryl was a leader; I was a follower, shy, a geek. My chief achievement to date had been teaching myself how to read and walk at the same time (ninety percent of the eyes on the page, ten percent of vision scanning the sidewalk for approaching humans, dogs, lampposts) and I walked to and from school each day reading and trying to pretend that I didn't really exist. I hated school. I was myopic but refused to wear my glasses, choosing instead to linger in my own blurred dimension. I knew I had something to hide, but I never really knew what it was. I had the feeling that I harboured some terrible, unspecified secret. If the other kids found out what it was, they would crucify me.

"You can be a vampire," said Sheryl. "The unquiet dead. Roaming the land, slaking your thirst."

It sounded good to me. We stole some plastic fangs and fake blood off her younger brother. Sheryl herself had decided to go as Casper the Friendly Ghost; we'd seen the movie together that summer. She donned a white sheet into which we sliced a couple of eye holes. We rehearsed our routine, a sort of good ghoul, bad ghoul thing; she would wave her sheet about a bit and ask 'trick or treat?' as politely as she could and, if our chosen victim seemed hesitant, I would start in with the fangs and the snarling. I liked the fact that I was the bad one; for us, it was a reversal of roles.

We were opposites, Sheryl and I. She was a bad-arse and I was frighteningly good, no trouble to anyone. My family, with its healthy living and its non-spanking policy, and its long talks around the dinner table every evening was boring, dull. We had no dramas, no fuming arguments. Nobody smoked, nobody drank. My parents were frugal; they had married young and money was tight. We grew all our own fruit and vegetables. Our curtains were made from sheets. Sheryl's parents weren't necessarily any wealthier, just freer with the cash. They had a trampoline, a colour TV, a soft-drink machine - all powerful lures for a young girl who came from a family where such luxuries were considered frivolous. My mother would pick fresh veges from our garden and whip us up a stir-fry. Sheryl's Mum would give her ten bucks and tell her to go get herself fish and chips for dinner and to bring back a packet of Rothmans. I didn't really know her father. He wasn't her real Dad anyway, she said, just a Step-Dad. She didn't know who her biological father was; she'd never met him. Her step-father wasn't home often but, in his own way, he made his presence felt. One day I went round to their house and Sheryl's mother had her arm in a cast.

"What happened to your Mum?" I asked.
"She fell off a ladder," came the reply. "She's clumsy, like me."
Sheryl's clumsiness was legendary. She often sported a number of dark bruises, blooming under her skin like the devil's roses.

On another occasion, her mother was vomiting in the backyard when I arrived. A strong sweet stench hung in the air, like the perfume of those roses that I had seen.

"What happened to your Mum?"
"Food poisoning."
Although I had a vague feeling that something wasn't quite right in this household, it was many years before I realised what was taking place, when everyone turned their eyes away, when

nobody looked; the drinking, the all too frequent walking into doors. The terror that Sheryl must have suffered in silence.

Sheryl was always daring me to do things I would not have found the courage to do on my own. She was fond of flaunting rules. For instance, I was only allowed to cross busy New North Road at the traffic lights up by the Mt Albert shopping centre. It was Sheryl who made me cross the road much further down, by her house – the road was so busy you could never get to the other side in one go, you always had to run to the middle and stand there with the cars speeding by on either side of you, waiting for a gap that would let you complete your crossing. The railway tracks were also on our way home. Sheryl didn't like to cross the tracks when it was safe. She would stand ten metres down from the designated crossing area, wait until the barrier went down and the bells started jangling and you could see the train approaching, and then she would sprint across at the last minute, right in front of the train. She liked to look death in the eye; it was how she got her kicks. Then there was the episode in the attic.

Sheryl lived in a similar style of house to mine; a 1920s wooden bungalow with big high ceilings, a roomy basement, a spacious attic. Solid wooden beams ran the length of the attic; between the beams was thin, relatively flimsy, plaster board which couldn't take much weight. In our attic, Dad had laid stronger planks from beam to beam in order that he could store boxes up there; unused crockery, his boyhood stamp collection, old photographs. My brother and I were sometimes allowed up there with my father. *Walk on the beams*, he would say, *walk on the beams. Remember June.*

The phrase 'Remember June' was a code. The previous June, Kane and I had been up there with Dad, who was doing some work on the wiring. My mother had been having afternoon tea with two of her friends in the living room below. Kane, awkward in his adolescent body, which seemed to change from day to day, hour to hour, minute to minute, had slipped off the beam he had been balancing on, gone crashing through the fibreboard and landed right in the middle of the living room floor. My mother's friends had got an awful fright, seeing my brother drop down from above in such a startling manner. Dad and I had nearly died laughing, but Kane and I both learnt the lesson well. *Walk on the beams.*

So I wasn't scared when Sheryl invited me up into her attic. Nobody else was home; we put a ladder up and scaled it rung by rung.

"Follow me," she said and, as always, I did.

Foot after steady foot we picked our way across to a brick structure that I failed to recognise as the chimney. Sheryl held two screwdrivers in her hand and showed me where she had been chipping away at the mortar. She had already created several small holes. She'd obviously been up here alone before, hiding or hanging out.

"It's really a job for two," she said, and she handed me a screwdriver.

We sat down on one of the beams and got to work, chipping away. Chip, chip, chip. The mortar seemed to fall away easily, it was satisfying work. I didn't think of it as vandalism; for me it was just a way to pass an otherwise uneventful afternoon. And, of course, it was a way to please Sheryl, to keep her happy. I didn't have many other friends; she was a twisted sort of a lifeline between me and total social ostracism.

Our activities may have pleased Sheryl, but they didn't please her family. The next time that they lit a fire the smoke flooded their entire attic. Luckily, the hatch that served as a gateway to the attic had been closed at the time, or they would have been smoked alive, like bees in a hive. Her dad had to pay a brickie to come round and repair the damage that had been done. They couldn't, for the life of them, figure out what had happened. Pigeons with razor sharp beaks, a cat with killer claws, mortar-chewing rats?

"It's not as if mortar *rots*," Sheryl's mother had said.

But we were never caught and we never confessed. Nobody knew that it had been us that had caused the 'flood' - us with our screwdrivers and our chip, chip, chipping.

The big night rolled around. I had convinced my mother to let me use her old Singer sewing machine in order to sew my own cloak. She had an electric sewing machine as well, but I wasn't allowed near that, she was afraid I would floor the pedal, lose control, sew my fingers, stitch myself to the fabric. The Singer, also, was not without its dangers, but at least, if it got me, it would be a slower sort of stab - she knew I would stop pedalling the minute I pierced myself; I wasn't a masochist. I bought a cheap piece of black fabric from a local store. I didn't have a pattern, I free-styled it, chopped a vague, cape-like shape, pinned and stitched it. I used bright red thread; although I searched all the drawers in my mother's sewing room, we appeared to have run out of black. I did prick my finger, towards the end, when I was getting a little too sure of myself as I finished off the hem; a light puncturing of the skin, a tiny globule of blood which I smeared across the cloak. I stashed the garment I had made in the back of the wardrobe until the hour when it would be needed. When the time drew nigh, I wrapped my mantle about my shoulders and headed out into the night.

A-haunting we will go. Sheryl briefed me before we set out for the evening.
"No apples," she said. "We don't accept apples."
She'd heard about people in the States putting razor blades inside. She drew a chalk circle on the ground and told me to step inside.
"What's that for?" I asked.
"Protection, stupid. Don't you know anything?"
She slung a black bag over her shoulder, a sack that we hoped would soon be filled with loot. We struck out, as thick as thieves, one of us cloaked in black, the other dressed in white. The fake fangs cut into my gums.
    Sheryl's street ran up the side of a hill; we started at the top and worked our way down. They weren't really prepared for us. No carved pumpkins graced windowsills to signify that goodies waited inside. Indeed, we had more than a few problems getting through to the locals. Nobody seemed to know what we were on about or, if they did, they feigned ignorance. The first door we knocked upon was opened by an elderly gentleman wearing a tweed jacket with corduroy patches on the elbows. I could hear *The Goon Show* playing on a radio in some other room of the house. Sheryl had positioned herself in the middle

of the doorway. I was off to the side; my plastic fangs and I were waiting in the wings.

"Trick or treat?" said Sheryl.

"Eh?"

"Trick or treat?"

"What do you mean, dear?"

I stuck one fang out over my lower lip, just to let him know that it was there, in case it was needed; a vague, meaningless threat.

"I mean," said Sheryl, putting one hand on her hip. "That you have to give us a treat, else we play a trick."

"Eh? A tree? I have to give you a *tree?*"

"No, a trea-*t*," said Sheryl, spitting out the last consonant.

"What kind of tree? I don't have many small ones, dear. Mostly just oaks and wattles and they've been growing on this property for decades. Their roots are ever so deep. Nothing I could dig up, dear, nothing I could dig up."

Sheryl changed tack.

"You have to give us something good - chocolate, mints, jellybeans, cash," she patiently explained. "Else we'll do something bad."

Our victim grew suddenly indignant.

"Goodness. Haven't children changed since my day. It used to be 'seen and not heard'. Now it's 'gimme or else.' Well I never, well I never. The impudence of it. I mean, *really*. Hilda! Come and get rid of these brats, would you?"

He shuffled off down the hallway and his wife appeared at the door with a fly swat in her right hand. She surveyed us as if with disdain.

"Go on, shoo," she said. "Go on. Get out of it. Scat."

She went at Sheryl with the fly swat, batting her about the ears. Sheryl screeched and backed down the steps. The two of us retreated to the street.

"We need to do something," said Sheryl. "Play a trick. Get revenge."

"What kind of trick?"

My imagination hadn't stretched that far. Sheryl whipped a black marker pen out of her pocket.

"You write on their door," she said. "That's what you do."

"What do we write?"

ALTERNATIVE MEDICINE | Laura Solomon

Sheryl thought for a bit.

"Misers," she said. "Let's write *misers*, like what your brother said about Jack."

"Ok," I said. "You do it, I'll watch."

"No *you* do it," she said, handing me the pen. "Go on. You need to prove yourself."

She didn't say to whom.

"Quick, before they come back to the door."

What could I do? I didn't want to lose face; I needed her approval. My hand was shaking so much I could hardly grip the pen. I climbed the porch steps and stood quaking before the door. *Misers*, I wrote, as quickly as I could, then shoved the cap back on the pen and sprinted across the street, where I hid behind a large oak and waited for Sheryl. She had taken a carton of eggs from her bag and was hurling them at the door, one by one, all six of them. They dripped and broke and slid down the wood. The broken shells lay on the doorstep like the fragments of somebody's mind. I was surprised by this outburst; I hadn't even known she'd had the eggs in her black sack. After egging the miser's door, Sheryl ran across the road and joined me. We crouched there for a while, two rioting spirits, hiding behind a tree. From where we were, peering out through the leaves, we could see the word that I had written. My handwriting, terrible at the best of times, had all its flaws intensified by the size of my script. Sheryl said that the 's' looked almost like a 'y'.

We didn't quit. The deaf man had been an unfortunate start, we reasoned. The evening would pick up from here. We did a number of streets, we knocked for several blocks. But the people who could hear us properly weren't much better than the deaf man. Nobody seemed to know what Halloween was; they weren't used to spooks knocking on their doors and making demands. They were unequipped to deal with it. They didn't even *fake* being scared; they just looked confused, mystified, pissed off that we had interrupted their evening. It took the wind out of our sails, having to explain to everyone the nature of our expedition. *You give us nice stuff, or else we get nasty.* After working most of the neighbourhood we totalled up our bounty; we had gleaned two small chocolate bars, a packet of wine gums and a can of peaches with the label peeling off. This wasn't the kind of reception we had been anticipating. I'd pictured the neighbours coming to the door with generous handfuls of sweets, maybe a cake or two, possibly a pavlova. That's what would have happened in America; why were we being punished just because New Zealanders were too clueless to figure out what was going on? Nobody had even tried to guess who we were beneath our masks. They just didn't seem to be buying it. We sat down together on the sidewalk, our feet in the gutter.

"I wish we lived in California," said Sheryl.

"Me too."

"Do you think, when I'm older, that maybe Tom Selleck might want to marry me?"

"Probably," I said. "No reason why not. You could go live in Hawaii. That'd be cool."

"Yea. Married to Tom Selleck and learning to surf. That's how I'd like my life to work out."

Sheryl surveyed our pathetic collection.

"Shall we give up and go home?" she asked.

"Yea," I said. "Let's call it a day. Or a night. Whatever."


My family moved cities; we always seemed to be moving. Sheryl and I wrote once or twice, and then we lost touch. I didn't hear of her again until many years later, when I was at university, studying law and, walking down the dormitory corridor one evening, I bumped into a girl who'd been to school with us.

"Hey," I said, after we'd made the usual preliminary chit-chat (I had, by this time, learnt how to fake social skills). "What ever happened to Sheryl? Do you remember her?"

"Sheryl Longely?"

"Yea, Sheryl Longely."

Was that her surname? I could barely remember it myself.

"She ran away from home when she was thirteen. Became a street kid. Then a hooker. Guy from our old school said he saw her on Karangahape Road one night, flashing her sorry wares. Poor soul. Wretched."

So, she had put herself up for sale. It was no great surprise. I remembered the bruises, the alcohol, the shadowy, absent step-father. I recalled the night that we had played at being two hungry spirits, prowling the hood, hoping for the gift of sugar and receiving, in its place, a cultural gap, misunderstanding. I thought also of poor Jack, unable to break into either heaven or hell, doomed to walk the earth for thousands of years, waiting for Judgement Day, when he could find his way home.

Printed in Great Britain
by Amazon

18516904R00109